Companion
Pieces

BOOKS BY
JONATHAN STRONG

Tike and Five Stories
Ourselves
Elsewhere
Secret Words

Companion Pieces

◆

Jonathan Strong

𝓩

ZOLAND BOOKS

Cambridge, Massachusetts

PUBLISHER'S NOTE

This book is a work of fiction. Names, characters, places, and incidents are either the product of the author's imagination or are used fictitiously. Any resemblance to actual events or locales or persons, living or dead, is entirely coincidental.

Portions of "Doing and Undoing" first appeared in *Triquarterly, Shenandoah, The Real Paper,* and *PsychCritique.* Portions of "Game of Spirit" first appeared in *Witness* and *Hanging Loose.*

FIRST EDITION

Text design by Boskydell Studio
Printed in the United States of America

This book is printed on acid-free paper, and its binding materials have been chosen for strength and durability.

Library of Congress Cataloging-in-Publication Data
Strong, Jonathan.
    Companion Pieces : two novellas / by Jonathan Strong.—1st ed.
    p. cm.
    Contents : Doing and undoing—Game of spirit.
    ISBN 0-944072-28-3 (acid-free paper) :
    I. Title.
PS3569.T698c6   1993
813'.54—dc20   92-43939
                                                             CIP

Companion
Pieces

Doing
and
Undoing

---◆---

for W. R. D. Rogers

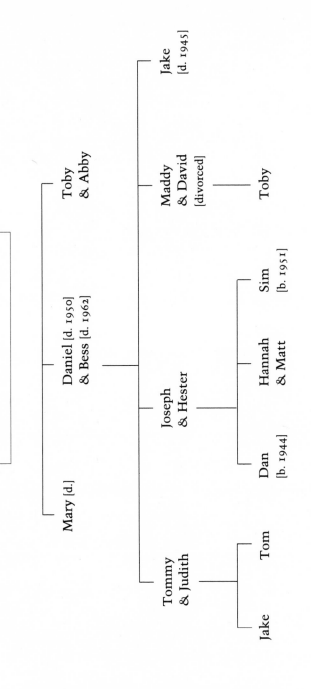

THE POORE FAMILY

Mary [d.]

Daniel [d. 1950]
& Bess [d. 1962]

Toby
& Abby

Tommy
& Judith

Joseph
& Hester

Maddy
& David
[divorced]

Jake
[d. 1945]

Jake

Tom

Dan
[b. 1944]

Hannah
& Matt

Sim
[b. 1951]

Toby

PART ONE

◆

Conversation
(Dan, Sim)

My dreams still take place here, most of them, half of them, over half.

Of the past? Memories?

But they take place now, with people as I know them now, and as I remember them too. We're sitting in familiar chairs, like these, in this big room, or standing at a window looking out. I recognize the contour of the land, the bluff down to the river, the stone wall along the top. Or I'm up in the tower, I fly out over all of this, no danger of falling, the peaky roofs and little turrets, the gardens, the pools, the river, the meadows. My dreams often take place in the meadow where we used to play. That's why I wanted to come see it all again.

I don't remember any dreams taking place here. I don't often remember my dreams.

I remember mine, many in a row, whole nights of dreams taking place here, one after another. I'm in that very gully off in the meadow. Or I'm on the edge of that very bluff, just such a slope, at just such an angle, with the river below.

Or I sense I'm walking down the lane of pines to that circle of trees in the woods, or to the lookout.

What I dream of is the sea, sailing, wind, storms, waves. Those are my kinds of dreams. I don't dream of back here at all.

You were too young when we left. You've mostly forgotten your first ten years. You didn't have things still around you to remember as you grew up.

I only dream of the sea, swimming, sailing. It comes to me in rhythms in my sleep, heaving and sinking, often not much more than that. Why don't I ever dream about you, my own brother? I don't know what I dream. There's a feeling of sea in them, storms sometimes, that's all I usually remember.

Back here there was only the muddy slow river. It rose in the spring up close to the highway. It used to scare me. I've dreamt about water slowly rising that way. Once the river washed over the highway a few inches. When we drove, our car seemed like a boat. Do you remember?

I was too young, maybe not even born.

But this morning I was amazed how you remembered the names of all the towns on the way.

I remember things I've memorized. We used to count the towns, I'll always be able to say them by heart, and then we'd start watching the bluff for the tower sticking up out of the trees.

How can you remember the towns and still never dream of back here?

I remember all the things I memorized then. I remember the capitals of the world. I remember the longest rivers and the largest seas, and all the flags of all the countries. You used to test me on them.

Do you remember the circle of trees in the woods? I often dream of being there late at night, afraid of being caught because I'm not supposed to be there. That's where I often snuck out late, in the dark. In fact, I should tell you, it's where I first made love, did you know that, Sim? Dreams must often take place in the place where you first made love. I might guess you first made love on the sea.

I'm not saying.

All right, I won't ask you. I dreamt about you recently in the gully in the meadow. It wasn't like it was. We were kids, but we were the same size, playing where I made my roads and towns and castles.

Wasn't that all supposed to be Tannu Tuva, your made-up country?

I didn't make up Tannu Tuva, but by then it didn't exist anymore. I found it on a map in our big old atlas from before the war. It was the most landlocked country in the world, farther from the ocean than any other country. The gully in the meadow was arranged sort of the way Tannu Tuva was, mountains rising on two sides, a river running through, the headwaters of the Yenisey.

The ninth longest river in the world.

In my dream we were being chased by wild boars. You wanted me to take you back to the house. I said I couldn't because although we were in the gully in Gramma's meadow, which we were pretending was Tannu Tuva, we were also in the real Tannu Tuva itself, and Gramma's house was on the other side of the world. In the dream you looked at me as your big brother, even if we were the same size. I was the one who had been places before you had, who remembered things before you could remember. I had this dream a few weeks ago, when I'd lost my job and I was already thinking about seeing if you'd take this trip with me.

Let's walk out and look at the gully this afternoon.

There's too much snow, Sim.

The real Tannu Tuva itself must be covered in snow now. It must be very cold there even in early spring. We could dig under the snow and see if one of your roads, or where a town was, was still there.

It's been years since Tannu Tuva was there. It's been years since I even saw the gully. The gully didn't keep its shape year to year. The water rushed down in the spring, washed everything away, on down the bluff to the river. Back then I couldn't recognize Tannu Tuva even the summer after I built it. It was contoured all differently. I did something else that summer. Hannah and I had one of our secret clubs. I only worked on Tannu Tuva on paper after that, maps, flags, the language, the history. Look, Sim, over there, do you remember that grate on the floor? Uncle Jake made a castle keep down there when he was a kid, in the heating duct.

Could we lift it off and look?

There's nothing to see. It's a pit, it's a huge duct, that's all. It goes straight down two floors to the basement. I was only down there one time, with Hannah. You were too young to go. We took a flashlight and climbed down by these iron rungs and crawled on our stomachs along the duct. Uncle Jake had left chains on the walls and handcuffs. We imagined things to be torture devices, places to put your head and get clamped in, and your legs could be stretched, and thumbscrews. I don't know if Uncle Jake made them to look like that or if we were just imagining. I felt it all around us in the dark, with light only at the top, and a voice coming down, Uncle Tommy yelling at us to get the hell out of there. I've never dreamt of the keep. It's the tower I dream about most often, and flying out from it, and sometimes of the river rising, sometimes of the wading pool with crab apples and leaves choking it. Do you remember that rotting boat with the boar's head carved on the prow that drifted in the wading pool?

I wasn't born then.

It leaked and scraped bottom. It had less paint every year. Pa finally dragged it out and planted flowers in it in the circle of trees in the woods.

I don't remember it.

Uncle Toby carved the boar's head. He carved the flowers and twisty vines over the doorways and over the windows. He painted the library ceiling and the imaginary coat of arms for the Poore family. We'll go and look at them and see if you remember.

Things come back to me when I see them. I remember feeling this was the biggest room I'd ever been in, bigger than any church. I remember that chandelier.

There should be one for the other end too. Uncle Toby carved the bodies out of a tree trunk. Our grandfather pounded out the iron arms in the forge. I used to think that's how he died, but he died back in the house, it was just that he'd been working in the forge that afternoon. The body of the unfinished chandelier used to be stored in one of the garages.

I'd like to stay here tonight instead of at Uncle Toby's.

You'd like to stay here, Sim, with a houseful of monks?

Maybe we could sneak back after dark and sleep in one of the garages, or the forge, in our sleeping bags.

I don't want to sleep here again. I don't even want to come here again, Sim, after today. This is the last time I want to see this place. I wanted to come here together and see it. I want you to remember it, so we can talk about it better. You're the only person I'd want to have come here with.

I wonder if some of Hannah's dreams take place here too.

What do we know about Hannah now? I don't think we know about her anymore.

Sometimes I don't know about you either, Dan. I didn't know what was happening about losing your job. It was a surprise you wanted to drive back here with me now. We might've never thought of it, never done it.

I almost didn't want to. I thought beforehand about not doing it. It seemed too much to do now. I was afraid of doing this sort of thing with you. We don't know about each other. And I wasn't really sure I wanted to see the place again. I don't mind that the monks are here now. They can afford to keep it, and we couldn't. But they take it all so seriously, did you notice, wanting to know what it was like to grow up here, spend our summers. I should've told them no one should be allowed to grow up in a place like this. You can't grow up in a place like this, a barn turned into a great hall, a silo into a tower, gargoyles stuck on, buttresses, turrets, a library out of a corncrib. I should have told them it was a huge extravagant playhouse for people who didn't take themselves very seriously. We only took it seriously when we were very little. I should've told them it was a good thing that the time when people could do this sort of thing is over. Back then people didn't think how these sorts of houses and pieces of land would have to go, or how families would move away from themselves. People don't really have a right to a place like this.

I want to go see if I remember the ceiling Uncle Toby

painted in the library. It has a peaked roof, doesn't it, all coming to a point?

♦

He liked to paint boars' heads. See that red boar's head? And all the boars on the coat of arms over the fireplace.

Do you think Uncle Toby's happy to see us again?

Don't you think so?

I was wondering at lunch if we were bringing back memories that made him sad.

I think he's happy to see us again, Sim. I'm glad we're staying there. Uncle Toby's house is a house on its own scale, not this sort of place.

Uncle Toby and our grandfather must've played games when they were little the way you and Hannah did. I was too young to go off with you and Hannah to track down capitalist spies in the woods. I never understood what you meant by capitalists. You used to say: Simmy, you can't come because we're tracking down capitalists, we're not just playing a game.

When I was little the Communist Manifesto was one of the first grown-up books I read. Hannah and I were Khrushchev and Bulganin. We liked them because they were funny fat men. I was Bulganin, because he was in charge when the game started, but Khrushchev got on top soon enough. Hannah always pretended to be Khrushchev when she drank her morning orange juice because he was off vodka at some summit meeting and drank only orange juice. We used all the characters, the rulers of the world, De Gaulle and Macmillan and Chou En-lai. Eisenhower and Nixon were always undermining something. Mir i Druzhba, we always said to each other. It's what Khrushchev said

at some summit meeting, Peace and Friendship. We loved
the Russians because they were supposed to be so evil. You
don't know what it was like back then, Sim. Communism
was the worst thing in the world. All the kids hated communism. We got Ma to sew us a Russian flag for our games.
She didn't want anyone to know she'd embroidered a hammer and sickle for her kids, but she did it for us. Ma and Pa
were the only Stevensonians in the family. Gramma wore
her little gold Eisenhower pin. We hated Eisenhower and
Nixon, and then after the election we decided to like Stalin
because he was their enemy. I remember pictures of him on
a balcony reviewing troops. He was made out to be very
scary in my childhood. When Ma and Pa went out for dinner
and we ate in the kitchen with Edna, she'd fill us full of
stories about Stalin. She called him Staleen. He was the
evilest person in the world. I started making up stories
about him when I was very small. Stalin was a great friend
of my Tannu Tuva, but of course in reality he had just
marched his troops in, it wasn't a country anymore. I didn't
know about that till we got the new atlas.

I didn't ever have anything like Stalin or Tannu Tuva. I
had my monkeys game, but I played that off by myself. I
didn't have anyone out here I liked to play with. I remember
how I used to go to Ma and say how I hated playing army
with Jake and Tom and I wished there were other cousins
my age. They were always making terrible lies and shooting
BBs and tricking each other.

At least you had boys to play with. I just had Hannah. Ma
told us never to let Gramma see our hammer and sickle flag.
It was bad enough we were for Stevenson. So we had our
secret meeting places up in the tower, or we'd sneak back in
here and into the chapel, the secret room behind the book-

case. It was just a storeroom, but we called it the chapel because Uncle Toby wanted to make it into a chapel someday so he could carve things for it, more gargoyles and little angels for the fun of it. It wasn't meant to be serious. Pa once told me he knew his father had considered himself a pagan. That's why Pa had to scatter Uncle Jake's ashes in the circle of trees in the woods and our grandfather's too, instead of having them buried. Pa couldn't bear to scatter Gramma's ashes though. Here, push on the bookcase. I'm sure Uncle Jake's secret button doesn't work anymore.

It's stuck.

Here, lift and push. It's wiggling. Wiggle it. There it goes.

Is there a light?

When Uncle Jake rigged it up, when he was a kid, he had it so when you pushed a button behind one of the books you heard chains rattling and strange thumps, and then the bookcase swung back with a creak. It still worked when I was little.

I remember coming back in here, but the button never worked.

You have to be careful to step only in the middle, where the boards are. This goes up over the archway.

There's a light.

There's a tiny window high up. What's in here now?

Piles of stuff. Mattresses.

It's just a storeroom, not a chapel. There's the old toboggan.

I'm surprised the monks haven't cleaned it up in here. Look at the old record albums, Dan.

Uncle Jake's. They're so heavy. I remember the way seventy-eights felt. I was always afraid of cracking them or breaking them. They spun around so fast. There was

Mozart's Thirty-eighth in a brown album and the Pastoral
Symphony in green. Pretty soon everyone had LPs instead.

I wouldn't listen to classical records when I was little.
And you didn't like my playing them all the time.

But nobody listened to classical records, no one else's
brother. You were the only person I knew who did.

I always made Hannah listen to my records. She liked
Paul Robeson singing spirituals best. Paul Robeson was
supposed to be a Communist back then.

There are lots of things in here, the toboggan, all these
records, maybe we should take some. We could fit a lot in
the station wagon.

I don't really want anything. I didn't want anything when
the house was sold. Everyone was supposed to pick the
things they wanted most.

That was the summer I went to camp. That's why I don't
remember things. The last time I might've seen them, I was
away and didn't. I'm sure I never came out here, Dan, after
Gramma died. I just remember Jake and Tom's army games,
and I didn't like coming out here except when I could be
alone, when we were the only family here, I wanted to play
my own games. You and Hannah liked playing together. I
liked playing by myself. Do you know what Uncle Toby said
this morning at lunch before you came in? What he remembered about me was that I liked to go sit under trees, and
once he asked me why I didn't want to go out to the meadow
and play games with Jake and Tom, and I said to him: Some
people like to go out to the meadow and play games, and
other people like to sit under trees and think.

People always asked me about you, Sim. They thought
you were in your own world.

You're the one who was off in your Tannu Tuva. I never
had that much of a world to be off in.

But I was busy making things up, very specific, lists of things, endless details. I didn't look thoughtful, I was too busy. It never went anywhere, of course. Being a child Stalinist didn't make me a radical in college. I played all those seventy-eights, but I couldn't stand piano lessons when I was small.

I don't think I used to think when I sat under trees. I just used to notice things. I liked to watch a bug crawling or study the shape of a leaf or listen for a bird. I was completely patient about it. I liked to feel sun on me. That could occupy whole minutes, concentrating on sun, or breeze, or looking at a square inch of land very closely, noticing what was on it. When I confined my watching to a square inch of dirt and grass, I'd see moving things I didn't first see. There were tiny red specks that moved on their own. There might be some twenty tiny specklike creatures I could see with my own eye on a square inch of land. I watched them move about. That's what I'd do under trees. It's what I liked about watching the sea when we moved east.

Do you know that I have a legal deed for a square inch of land near Nome, Alaska, that I actually own in my name? You could get a square inch of land through some cereal box top. The only land I own in the world is a square inch in Alaska, covered with snow. I have the deed in my desk in my apartment.

Let's go back into the library, Dan. We don't want any of the stuff here anyway.

I'd like to look through these record albums. No, but I don't really want to, I'd never play them. You have to change seventy-eights every five minutes, and they sound so crackly. I don't even play the old Paul Robeson records, I'm too used to playing LPs. Once in a while I'll play one, if I get a special twinge of a memory. There's a certain feeling about putting on those heavy breakable records and having them spin so fast. Each year when we were small, back when you were still a baby, Hannah and I would have our secret Christmas ceremonies. We'd make a chapel out of a card table and a quilt draped over it and put the old Victrola in there and bring in all our stuffed animals, the Tannu Tuvans. We'd pretend that our friend Stalin was there too. We played all the Christmas carols on old seventy-eights. The ceremony always came to an end with Paul Robeson. Peter Whoaboat, my rabbit, Stalin's great friend and ally, Prime Minister of Tannu Tuva, he'd get up and sing. Let's go back to the library, Sim. It's musty in here.

◆

I do remember sitting on this couch in a rainstorm. I suddenly remember it very well. I don't remember the coat of arms or the sliding bookcase as well, but I do remember cuddling up in a quilt on this couch, and you and Hannah were playing records, and studying. It must've been early fall, when Gramma hadn't yet gone back to town and just our family was here with her for a weekend. Maybe that's my last memory of being here, the fall she died. I remember the musty orange velvet of the couch. There was wild wind outside. The music you were playing was like a storm.

Probably Mahler, that was my Mahler period. Gramma couldn't stand Mahler. She'd make us leave the concert if Mahler was played. It was too loud and long for her. Do you remember Gramma at all when she was dying?

I remember her in her wheelchair and how we'd go up and touch her when we came in the room after she was blind so she'd sense us more than just by our voices.

I loved that.

I did too.

It's the only memory I have of touching Gramma. She was icy otherwise. Ma used to talk of how icily withering she could be to a daughter-in-law.

What did she say about Gramma? I'd like to know more about Gramma because I was only ten. Before she was in her wheelchair I don't remember much. I remember her once going for a swim in the big pool with us grandchildren.

Did you know she was a music student in college? She hated the old ladies who came in late to the Friday afternoon concerts and whispered during quiet moments. Gramma took music seriously. She'd give them withering stares. She had her opinions. That's why she'd walk out on Mahler. It wasn't that it was too modern for her. She liked lots of modern things. But she didn't feel music should be as long and as tortured. Of course I loved Mahler most of all. He overwhelmed me. He was my secret dream music. I remember the talk we had when she was blind in her wheelchair. It was after Hannah and I were too old for our games. I knew Gramma was dying, and I wanted to spend time with her. I thought I was her favorite grandchild. I was the oldest, and I was named after our grandfather and I thought she saw me as being like Uncle Jake, while cousin Jake wasn't like Uncle Jake at all. I listened to music the way Uncle Jake had. He hadn't kept up piano lessons either. He never played anything but the Victrola, like me. I used to think she saw me as being like him. I was afraid of her, but I liked her best when I could talk with her and even argue with her about music. Maybe Mahler was too much a member of her own parents' generation for her. But then maybe she was already just an impatient, cold, suburban rich woman who was bored by long symphonies with so much nightmarishness in them.

I don't know anything about these things.

Well, Sim, it's not important, we couldn't resolve our

argument anyway. She would get a bit excited when we talked and say: Danny, I wish I'd live long enough to see your tastes change! And then, being more serious: To see you change—it's terrible to think, Danny, of only seeing you up to sixteen, oh, maybe I'll see you up to seventeen or eighteen, even though of course she had already stopped seeing me with her eyes. She'd last seen Uncle Jake when he was eighteen. I do feel she saw me as him. In all the times we talked, that was the only time, in just one sentence, when she ever said something about her dying to me. I probably don't remember it exactly as she said it, but it was something like: Danny, it's terrible to think of only seeing you when you're sixteen, or maybe eighteen at most. When I used to come in I'd always say first: Gramma, it's Danny, and go to her wheelchair and touch her wrist and perhaps pat her hand, and she'd say: Sit down, dear, I'm not too tired, glad you came in. I remember the room with the old beds with spindles in the headboards, country-style, and quilts with little pink tufts dotting them. The sun came in from the windows on the garden side, along the bluff. It wasn't like her bedroom in town with canopies and ruffles and heavy curtains.

Her bedroom in town is where I saw Gramma last when she was dying. She was very tiny on the chaise longue, and I went out crying.

I remember you crying then, Sim. I was worried about little Sim crying. When we were out in the car going back to our house, you were all choky and said: Gramma looked so small, Gramma looked so small, when I touched her she was so light.

And I'd remembered Gramma as being big. I wish I'd been old enough to have talked to her privately the way you did.

But why do I think of her as icy cold, Sim? I remember how we talked, and I know she loved me, but I think of her as icy. I remember the times she'd come to our house for dinner, seeing the Packard pull in the drive, or when it would pull in the drive to pick us up for the concert, it was almost a scary thing, Gramma inside it in back. We could only touch her when she was blind and we wanted her to know we were there.

I remember when Gramma came to swim in the pool. It seemed wonderful that she was coming to swim with us, a special occasion. She used to call me Simmy. I was probably called Simmy by everyone then.

I always called myself Danny to her. I think she was beginning to call me Daniel at times. I wonder if I remember going to her room to sit and talk about music because I want to think of her as wise and artistic. I wonder if back then, despite my arguing, I secretly believed she was right about clear, formal music, and that I was too romantic and overwhelmable to appreciate the clarity yet, and that by listening to her talk I was growing up somewhat. I can make her into quite a figure in my mind when I want to. Aunt Maddy once said she didn't think Gramma loved music at all. She thought Gramma had a certain taste, she approved and disapproved. She said how Gramma was almost embarrassed by this house. For every piece of plain country furniture she found for it, our grandfather would find something grand, those throne chairs, or Uncle Toby would go carving vines and flowers over doorways and painting the ceilings with boars or crenellating walls, or her youngest son Jake would make a secret passageway somewhere. That's why she kept the house only for the family. This wasn't a place to show but go hide in. She hid over the summers. She drew all the family in around her and hid. She'd go back to town in the fall when the concerts began.

Aunt Maddy doesn't think Gramma loved music?

Aunt Maddy's bitter about Gramma at times. She had to go through things Pa and Uncle Tommy and Uncle Jake never did, the sorts of things daughters had to do back then, even her marriage, until she was finally able to get off to the woods. There's no way of knowing how Gramma felt about music. She was mysterious. How did she really feel about this house, or feel about me? Approval or disapproval, matters of taste, what Aunt Maddy said. She'd wear her Eisenhower pin and stare icily at Ma's Stevenson button, she'd walk out on Mahler. Ma got into an argument once with her about Paul Robeson. To Ma, Paul Robeson seemed a tragic great man. She would never argue with Gramma, but when it came to Paul Robeson she couldn't restrain herself. It's the only explosion of Ma's I ever saw. She threw a book across the room, then she went off and cried. Of course, Gramma would never reveal any racial prejudice, but Paul Robeson was a Communist, she said. Whenever Ma showed any sympathies that way, Gramma would set her withering stare on her. Ma was easily withered. So were the chatty ladies in the next box at the concert. Gramma would cast her great withering stare if they coughed in a quiet moment. You know something that shocked me after she died? I was looking through her files, helping Pa clear things up, and I found a paper she'd presented to her club on the Black Hawk War. I read the paper and then looked through some of her history books because I got interested, and I found essentially the whole paper, word for word, in one of her books. And I'd always been so impressed that Gramma was scholarly, at her age, writing papers on local history. I didn't mention what I'd found to Pa. I felt odd knowing Gramma had done something like that. Hey, Sim, I've been talking and talking and you haven't said anything.

I want to hear these things. They're things I've never heard. There's nothing I can really say because I don't remember any of this.

But you must remember some things. You remembered Gramma going swimming, you remembered how small she was when she was dying. What else do you remember? You remembered sitting on this couch.

I remember sitting on this couch, musty orange velvet, with you and Hannah playing records and studying over at the table. Seeing you and Hannah study made me think you knew things I would never know, read books I never would, and you understood music I would never understand. I used to watch both of you a lot. You did things I couldn't understand. Not just when you wouldn't let me go track down capitalist spies, but all the things you did, the games, the studying. You didn't pay attention to me much.

You always liked being left alone.

I did like it, but I think I grew to like it because I found myself often left alone. I grew to like watching the square inch of ground, but I never studied the things I liked to watch, I just watched them. And now next year I've got this job teaching sixth grade, but I'm not sure it's what I want to do with myself. You think I know what I'm doing because I went on and got an M.A. and got a job, but I might have gone off like you did, quit school, tried myself fresh, alone.

You've considered that.

But I won't next year. I have this job. I have to see what it's like.

I could use your job. Give it to me, and you go off to sea, how's that!

I'd never go off to sea.

What are your sea dreams like? Tell me more about them, Sim. Are they nightmares mostly?

I just dream of sea and storms. I don't think of them as nightmares. I'm thinking of them now because of being on this couch, remembering that wild storm outside, very dark for the middle of the afternoon, your storm music on the Victrola, you and Hannah reading seriously at that table, me wrapped in one of those tufted quilts you remembered from Gramma's room. I remember them, big fluffy things, slightly musty smelling, with little pinkish tufts of yarn I'd twiddle with. There was probably a fire in the fireplace. I remember tree branches whacking at the windows. I remember always being afraid of those woods out there. I used to have nightmares of bears coming out of those woods and breaking into my room when I was sleeping alone in the small room beside Ma and Pa's room.

You do remember things about back here. You do remember dreams that aren't just sea dreams.

I vaguely remember the fear of bears in the woods. I don't know if it came in dreams or if I had it when I was awake, trying to fall asleep, and no one else was in that wing of the house.

Didn't you always sleep with your Dotted-Swiss bear?

Dotted-Swiss didn't help against real bears though.

There probably haven't been real bears in these woods since Black Hawk's time.

These woods in a storm were frightening. They tossed all around the house. That time I was wrapped in the quilt on this couch I was very drowsy. It was partly comforting to have my big brother and sister sitting there at the table, with a light between them, and music going. I'm surprised I didn't get to know music, just hearing it from you. I closed it out. It was something you did.

Hannah closed it out mostly too. She said it helped her study because it kept her mind from wandering. Hannah used to have terrible eye aches. I remember her always pressing her eyes, and I would think she was crying. She hated studying.

I never read, Dan, I never listened to music. I never got to go to the concert with Gramma.

I was always afraid of going up to the edge of her box. You had to sit on straight chairs right at the front. The railing was low in front. I was afraid of falling forward, even just of dropping my program down onto some white head below. Sometimes I dream of concerts. I dream whole performances of pieces I've never heard. I wonder what I actually hear in my dreams. I wake up feeling I've heard music, music I haven't heard before. Perhaps I'm composing in my sleep. When I used to mow lawns, to earn money to buy records, I'd sing whole made-up symphonies in my head, even out loud sometimes under the noise of the mower, all off-key, no one could hear me. I'd write down whole lists of pieces I'd made up mowing lawns. I attributed them all to a composer I invented, that was one of my favorite diversions, I wrote his biography, I wrote analyses of his works. I never tried to learn to compose in reality. It was one of my secret games.

You always had your games, Dan, secret from me.

You had your plastic monkeys game though, whatever it was. I didn't mind you playing it around me, as long as you didn't wreck anything like smudge my roads and bridges or

crawl through my towns. You were never a troublesome kid.
I let you play up on the edge of the gully while I made Tannu
Tuva. And Hannah and I would play with you, wheeling you
around on our Stevenson Bandwagon when you were only a
baby. We draped crepe paper around you and sat you in the
wagon. Or was that one of the Tannu Tuvan coronation
ceremonies and we put a crown on you?

The plastic monkeys were like explorers. They went on
expeditions through unexplored territory. I'd like to be out
in the meadow or in the woods with them exploring, but on
their small scale. They were only an inch high. I'd be down
on my stomach marching them along through the grass.
Once in a while you'd come do something with me. I always
felt good about it, but slightly scared. We didn't do much
together.

When did you stop feeling scared of me?

At times I still feel scared of you, when I feel I don't know
you, when I'm afraid you're mad at me, when you don't tell
me things, like about your job, or about Miriam.

Then this trip is good for us. If we could stand sitting in
that car for a thousand miles, and coming out here and
seeing all this again, we must be getting better as brothers.

It's when I think you don't particularly think of me as
your brother that I get scared of you.

But I always think of you as my brother. I really love you,
Sim. I love you more than anyone else in the family. That's
how it's turned out, now that we're grown up.

All right, Dan, I'm not afraid to say I love you too, you're
the only person I trust, that's true, but sometimes I think
you don't particularly think of me as your brother, your
mind's on something else, sometimes I don't trust even you.
I have a hard time trusting anyone. I get feeling empty

quickly after I say something that I think I mean. I wonder what I meant by it. I say something like I love my own brother and that I trust him, and it's not untrue, but I feel empty quickly, right away. I think I'm always going to be by myself. I'm afraid of loving even you. I like going sailing with a few friends, I play tennis with people, we have our pickup soccer games Sundays, it's all fun, I like those people, but they won't be there next year. I feel easily tossed about by whoever's there and organizing things at the time.

Did you feel I organized this trip too much?

I thought I should do it. I was a little afraid of spending so much time with you.

I was hesitant a little, Sim, too. But after figuring out what to do with Miriam, and I admit my mind was mostly on that, and I didn't think of you, but I knew I had you to come to, you were the one I'd be able to come to. I've never had anyone else like that.

Driving was good. There had to be lots of silences. I got used to not having to say something to you all the time.

You never used to feel you always had to say something to me.

When I was smaller I could just sit to one side and watch you and Hannah. The memory of being on this couch is so strong. Being here makes me feel drowsy. I almost want to leave.

I'm on the couch too, I'm not over at the table studying. Hannah's not here, there's no storm music, there's no wild storm outside. It's cold, crusty snow, sunny woods, you can see way into them. They seem like thin, bare woods now.

It's open and bare now. What I remember is darkness and leaves whipping off the trees and swirling around, tree branches whacking against the windowpanes. This isn't the way I remember being on this couch at all. And I had fevers and chills then and had to stay wrapped in the quilt. Now it's just that my fingers are chilly from the cold, my nose is full of the mustiness, but I don't feel sick. It's just the drowsiness, the couch's softness. I feel a little dizzy. We've been talking too much about things. When I start talking about how I feel, I get dizzy, I want to stop talking. I even feel sick to my stomach when I try to explain what I mean. It can't be explained. Talking doesn't do any good. I feel empty and stupid and cold. I feel I want to listen to you talk and talk about the past and learn things I never knew and try to remember things, but I don't want to talk myself, I don't want to tell you anything about what I remember, I'm afraid you're going to want to know too much about me, that all your talking about what you remember has to be answered by my talking about what I remember, and I don't remember. I remember vaguely the monkeys in the long grass, I remember vaguely avoiding Aunt Judith when she wanted me to play with Jake and Tom, I remember vaguely Gramma when she was blind, her going swimming, when I was sick on this couch. Vaguely. I'm making up what I remember about it all. It's just a feeling I remember that I'd like to have sharp memories for. I'd like to imagine I can see exactly how you and Hannah were over there, feel exactly the storm, all the tossing and heaving and sweating and freezing, the feeling of not knowing at all who you and she were, knowing that Gramma was dying, would be going back to town soon, that I'd never gone to the concerts with her the way you had, that I never would know those things, know this place because it was going to be gone. I absolutely knew it was going to be gone. You didn't know it the way I knew it.

What made you know it?

I knew nothing would stay. I always knew that, even when I was small. I would never get to do the things you and Hannah had. They would be gone by then.

Sim, I don't want you getting upset.

You get upset seeing this place because of all it means to you. I get upset talking about it all because it doesn't mean anything to me. You know this place, you dream about this place. I don't dream about anything, just blind darkness, tossing, heaving. I don't feel anything. I only say I love you because you're my brother and I know it's not untrue, but I don't know how it's true.

I won't let you say that, Sim.

Why?

Because you've been talking with your voice shaking, sitting on the edge of the couch, and you're desperate to convince me you don't feel anything. What have you been talking about then? Why are you so upset? I won't let you say you must love me because I'm your brother. I won't let you. You know what? I don't love Hannah the way I once did, I don't love Ma and Pa the way I once did either, I'm coming not to love even the memory of Gramma. I love all of them still, but I don't feel engaged with them, either now or as I remember things, and I don't feel them engaged with me. You don't have to love people because you're related to them. But I know I love you because we're talking to each other this way, and you said you weren't afraid to, I'm the only person you trust, you're the person I've come to.

I haven't been able to cry about anything for a long time. I don't remember ever being able to cry about anything. I last cried a long time ago.

Are you about to cry now?

No.

Your eyes are starting to. Look at me.

I can't cry. You asked me where I first made love. What did you want to know? What did you mean by make love? What's that? Doing what looks like making love? What if I've never made any love, I've never actually made love, created love, made it in the sense of creating it, made something that wasn't there before? I've never done that at all. You and Miriam made love. You did make love. I know you made love, even if it wasn't quite enough love. Any amount is more than none.

You have to start at it, Sim.

I can't start at it.

Anyone can start. You certainly can start at it.

I don't have the sources of it inside me.

What sources?

Memories of it, dreams of it. How can you make something you have no dreams of?

Of course you have. You don't have to know what it is yet.

You have to have some inkling.

Where do I get my inkling? I wonder if I have these sources of love either.

You loved Tannu Tuva, you loved the music you made up mowing the grass, you loved Stalin and Peter Whoaboat, and being Communists with Hannah. You made up countries that didn't exist, made languages, made music in your head, you made up the person who made the music.

It was in my head, I haven't ever actually made it.

You have.

I haven't made it for anyone else. What we're talking about has to be for someone else too. I had to learn. It's only lately I can say I learned to love you even. Do you think I made love, the way you're talking about it, the first time? I can't say I've made it even yet. I began to make it more with Mir, you're right, but it wasn't enough, for either of us. I've been trying seven years longer than you have, and what have I made? How do you think I was when I was twenty-three? So what if I took off from things, and you stayed dutifully in school and went through it all and will get your M.A. and your job.

I'm more afraid than you were.

How do you know? What did I do when I took off? How much time did I spend staring at walls and lying on my back thinking no thoughts or drawing detailed contour maps of valleys in Tannu Tuva with every little shepherd's cottage inked in? My friends thought I must be some sort of odd genius, of course, but all those damn maps are in a file cabinet in the bottom of my closet, and they're of no interest to anyone, including me. And the lists of the complete works of Timothy Usk, that was his name, the composer I made up who'd written the music I sang to myself, those lists, that biography, the themes I jotted down are all in that file too. All that time and energy, tremendous energy, uselessness, more of my secret games.

But listen to you go on about them. You still get excited about them. You love them.

They still have a pull on me. I'm drawn to them. They excite me.

I think they're part of the sources of love inside you.

You have them too, Sim. I want to shake you almost, till they come out.

You're mad at me.

I can get mad at you. It's better than withering stares. You're mad too. Look at me. You're mad at me too.

No, stop it, Dan, I don't want to talk like this anymore. Let's go up to the tower. I don't want to be in here anymore. Sometimes I get so mad at you I'd like to smash you, when you start telling me how things are. You figure it all out. You rise above it right away. You try to make me look at you and say what I mean, and that's the worst way, that's when I won't do anything.

I'm sorry, Sim. I still feel I have to tell you things like an older brother. I'll try to stop. We're not used to talking to each other about these things.

I don't like being told things, or talking about things about myself, with anyone.

I'm sorry, Sim, for being older brotherish. I don't mean to be. I don't like it when I am. I want to be the same as you, not overbearing like that, but I get going. We don't have to talk for a while. Do you want to go up to the tower? We can just look out from there, not have to talk.

We can stay here for a while now if you want. It doesn't bother me. I was uncomfortable about it for a moment. I had the feeling you were making me tell you about everything. What I really want to do is just sit here for a while, but not talk.

It sounds like one of the monks is practicing the organ in the great hall, hear it, the low pedal notes? I used to pick out tunes on the pedals and make the walls shake.

We can go up to the tower in a bit, but let's sit here a bit more first. I want to have it the way it was in the car, not feeling we have to say anything.

Sim's Thoughts

Not say anything, musty orange velvet, the frayed edge of the cushion, Dan breathing in gasps, an edge of cold slipping through the window frame behind us, he is looking at the peak of the ceiling, vague memories of marching my monkeys through the grass and setting them up to guard frontiers, exploring tiny new territories, certain patches of grass, Dan breathes in gasps, looking at the ceiling, the red paintings of wild boars, his old games with me, well-trained little Simmy who can tell the longest rivers and widest seas, the capitals of the world, playing on the edge of the gully, do I remember because he talked about it or do I actually remember, he is down there driving toy cars over tiny roads, I am too young to remember, do not remember, cold slipping about my fingers, touch the tips to my cheek, touch the velvet, sink into the couch, heaving seas and storms, not say anything, of course I first made love on a boat, he did guess, do not want to remember anything, why does Dan brag of his memories, proud of the clever things he thought up, I do not like to hear about them, I hear his gasps, do not look over at him, close my eyes, cheek against the velvet, against the ground watching troops of monkeys marching slowly through, emerging around grass clumps, ladybugs crossing their paths, smaller bugs, dots only, tiniest moving things on a square inch of land, watching monkeys one by one step around a clump, on down tiny paths, an hour spent moving an expedition, stationing itself in the branches of a bush, the lookout, the edge of unexplored territories, down into a gully, I could not take them down there, why does

Dan ask where I made love, I said I never made love in one sense, believe I cannot, have never attached it to my life, he never saw me with anyone or bringing anyone home to meet the family, I want to make them all curious about me, tell them nothing, not say anything, Dan is breathing, sleeping, making up something clever in his mind, they have the family that goes on about me but does not bring me in, they were all there before me, the cold edge slips through the window frame, the top of my head is cold, I am an after-thought, wish they would admit they had not planned me, they do not want me not to feel loved, did say I loved Dan, have never said such a thing to someone in my family, not even when I was small, Ma and Pa have said it to me at times, I do not know what they meant, must know what I mean when I say it, mad at Dan for his memories and braggings and how he goes on and does not listen to me but wants to tell me things and wants me to tell him things too but only by him shaking them out of me and not waiting for me to say what I want to say, said too much, do not want to say anything for a while, when we moved east I never thought of this place again, did not want to remember it, should I remember my first ten years, I had to play with Jake and Tom and storm around through the woods breaking branches and throwing stones over the bluff and watching them break off small avalanches, some like to play games and others like to sit under trees and think, I stayed a bit behind, would run back to the house to get pop for them, Jake smashed a pop bottle down the bluff, what if Gramma had found out when she was blind, no one told her, I was afraid of Gramma, she was stern with me and she was blind and dying, the fear not that she would die but that she was dying in front of my eyes over months, she was now a quarter dead, she was now half dead, she was over half dead, memories, of the past, I never dream of her, do not remember what she looked like except in pictures, remember her swimming in the pool with us, she made a few laughs, poked at me, I do not remember doing that, she made the dotted-swiss skirt for my bear, not a boyish thing for me to have had, a bear who is there, I said that once to Ma, I always said it, a bear who is there, I was shorter than Dan, his hand was bigger than mine as we held the bear, now our hands are the same size, look at his wrist, his fingers look cold, they do not move, he is not looking at the ceiling, does not know I am looking at him, caught glimpses over at him when he was driving, his eyes on the road, his eyes staring forward now, not asleep, he is thinking, he is my brother, I am always nervous with him, do not know what to say, have to keep thinking of things to say, ways to keep him from getting at things I do not want to say to him, if we were to sleep here tonight in our sleeping bags out in one of the garages, out in the forge, the monks would not know, if I am to dream of this place, heaving sea, I may dream of it when I go back east, I may never dream of it, I dream of sea and sky, I dream but I do not remember what I dream, if I were to make Dan listen to me, if I were to start telling him things and running the conversation the way he runs it, if I were to make him shut up and listen to me only, to ask me questions but say nothing of himself, could I make him hear things my own way without him understanding them, make him confused, keep him from having answers or figuring out what I mean, do not know what he means when he goes on about music, do not even listen to him, he keeps talking, talks about made-up countries, what if I started talking the way I think and made him see how it could make no sense to him then he might leave me alone and not try to understand me, I know I have gone all wrong, he wants to understand and help, I do not want him to understand because he cannot and cannot help, do not believe anyone can help, tired of him pointing out how I might work at things, I do not think Dan is interested in me, he is curious about me but not interested, I sink into the couch, wrap myself up in the quilt which is no longer here, pinkish tufts on the quilt, stuffing coming out of it, no bears in these woods since Black Hawk's time, I saw a bear at our campsite at summer camp, not afraid of real bears, not afraid of storms, love to sail in high wind, will take a boat out in wild waves, only afraid when I dream, dreams are overwhelming, placeless, of course I first made love on my boat, we were down in the cabin quickly, rocking, anchored in the cove, not my idea, found it nothing terrifying, he did not know who I was, did not know him, he had been at the beach, not from one of the regular families, someone's cousin maybe, once with him, once with that other boy, and someone else on the beach once, or anchored in the cove, down in the cabin quickly, rocking, sloshy sounds, tippy, not the heaving sea of dreams, the awkward ins and outs and trying to keep from rolling off the little bunk and not having enough room and banging my head, and having my bathing suit tangled at my feet, it was nothing very terrifying, enjoyed it, we laughed about it, decided to do it again sometime, but with someone else instead it turned out, did not see him again either, do not want to do things again, did not want to come back here on this trip, afraid of Dan, did not want to sit beside him in a car for a thousand miles, did not want to explain to aunts and uncles what I was doing with my life, not say anything, the boy whose name I do not know, not the first time for him, do not know where the others are, played tennis with people I do not ever see again, the shape of the beach has changed, my cove is not as much of a cove, the beautiful fiberglass of my boat, corduroy cushions leaving lines on his back and on my knees, we laughed about it, I laughed when he laughed, if we could have been farther out at sea on a great swell, swam afterwards without our suits, not gone long, sailed back while the sun was still setting, I took that boy who was visiting next door out for a sail, sort of nice, a little afraid of sailing, the wild way Sim sails says Pa, no one else was much on sailing, why did we move to the beach, Ma played tennis but I was too good for her, Pa never played anything, Dan never played anything, Hannah had eye aches, pressing her eyes, studying, look at the warp of the table from the dampness, where they used to sit, want to look at Dan but do not, put my cheek against the soft musty velvet, the corduroy bunk left stripes on my knees, on his back, on his bottom, on my elbows, we noticed it even in the growing dark, long summer sunset, much colder my second time, we had blankets, anchored in same place, did not swim, did not laugh, sailed home together quietly, odd feeling, Ma and Pa careful never to ask me questions about what I did, Hannah was already married, Dan lived with Miriam, Ma and Pa would talk to me about Dan, would not talk to me about me, much time telling me what they worried about over Dan, did not trust Miriam, they made me not like her, she was not friendly with me, silly younger brother, playing tennis, sailing, saw her at meals, did not talk, Ma and Pa knew I did not like her, Dan and Miriam's big double bed when I visited them, bigger than Ma and Pa's, I slept on narrow couch in other room, Miriam was nice when I visited, if I had had my own friend to be with, never seen me living with anyone, if I had a brother nearer my age to discuss it with, I have no friends, never keep a friend more than a year, there will be different people to play soccer with next year, have had different friends every year, I would like one best friend to keep and depend on, Dan is my best friend, wish he was, could be, he does not tell me anything, did not know he lost his job, what will Dan ever do, he has never liked any of his jobs, does he ever see Miriam now, did not tell me when they stopped living together, Ma and Pa said be nice to Dan, he must be having a hard time now, first I had heard of it, probably for the best but he will not think so now, we have to understand his moods, what about me, must talk to Dan about Ma and Pa, mad at them, do not want me to love anyone, I am the one who has done what they want, have not gone abroad to live, have not lived with some woman they did not like, have not brought anyone home even, out around the point, too quick to suspect it, never stayed out late, not off with friends, I am always smaller, I am smaller on this couch, I sink in, mustiness, velvet, I must say something, Dan, not out loud, he is asleep, thinking, imagining, not break his thoughts, Dan sets things going, organizes, do what Dan says, wait for Dan, I came because I want to become his friend now, he is different from me, he is right that you do not love someone because they are in your family, I said I loved him but do not know, is he awake, Dan, no, not say anything, the frayed edge of the cushion, wrapped in the quilt, freezing, sweating, dizzy, think myself into it, small, smaller than he is, remember, he never paid attention, hung crepe paper on me for his bandwagons, his coronations, had me memorize capitals of the world, play on the edge of gully, leave him alone, I would not understand, they had to chase capitalist spies, what is spies, not tell you, get us some pop, would get pop, drink green pop by the pool, paddled about, Jake and Tom doing cannonballs and splashing Aunt Maddy, Uncle Tommy telling them to get the hell out of the pool, Gramma in the pool once, blue and white flowery bathing suit, the skirt fluttering in the water, remember it, she poked me, did she poke me, think back to it, it is dark outside, there is crackly storm music on Dan's Victrola, branches whacking at the window behind me, wrapped in the quilt, feverish, chilly, sink into the couch, lamp on the table, Dan and Hannah studying under it, Hannah's fingers pressed to her eyes, Dan writing away, warm under the lamp, dark in this corner, a whirl in the woods outside, Gramma is dying, half dead, over half, this is the last day in the house, end of summer, she will die in the fall, I will go to summer camp next summer, will split up the house without me, the last day in the house, am I thinking of the right one, I do remember it all, Dan is beside me, Hannah is in England, fingers pressed to her eyes, my fingers are cold, under the quilt, I am smaller, deep in the couch, not seen, asleep, crackly old record, edge of cold, I am very afraid of all this, alone at night in my room, others still up, playing Scrabble, talking, I am in bed early, summer, windows open, screens, wind in trees, noises in woods, a shadow at the window, the bear who is there, there is where the bear who is there is, Hannah would say whar is the bar who is thar, would laugh with me, left Dotted-Swiss all night once at the edge of the woods under a tree, forgot her, she sat all night under tree, when I woke up I ran about crying till I remembered where she was, dew covered, why do I never remember when I was a child, the last day in the house, no one here but us, our family helping Gramma close

up for the winter, wheeled Gramma about in the wheelchair, this big house empty all winter, the heating ducts
unheated, sheets over things, mothballs, checked all the
windows, closed the flues, went around with Pa and Dan
checking, I do remember, the weekend I was sick on this
couch, Hannah and Dan had homework to do, I did not, that
would come next year in sixth grade, I am an afterthought,
stop thinking that, stop breaking into my thoughts, cannot
concentrate on anything, do not want to remember anything of this place, why do I want to remember, I feel sick to
remember Dotted-Swiss covered with dew in the morning,
feverish, why do I not want to remember Hannah and Dan
doing homework, Dan always played his records loud, record after record, no silence, I need silence, if the monk
would stop playing the organ, the walls shaking with it, the
house shaking, shaking me, I do not have to tell what I am
thinking, why does he want to know where I first made
love, if he could trust me without knowing anything, if he
could always be there, he must be thinking about me, never
think anyone is thinking about me when I am thinking
about them, think I always think about other people, no one
thinks about me, why do I think that, I always went out
sailing alone, way beyond the point, almost could call it the
high seas, I imagined it was, close my eyes, take down sail,
down in the cabin, heaving, imagine all things, favorite
place for beating off, no one for miles, part of Jake's army
games was beating off, remember that, I did not know what
it was, Tom did know but he was younger than I was, he
loved to watch Jake do it, I never watched, would not tell
anyone, go get us some pop, if Gramma knew, Dan always
played with Hannah, never knew about Dan beating off,
when I knew what it was he had gone to college, I did not

want anyone to know anything about me, Ma and Pa never asked me questions about anything I did with anyone, younger one who did not have to do things, watch a certain patch of grass, watch my big brother and my big sister, and my Gramma would poke me in the pool, I must remember that, it must have happened, must love my childhood, must love this place, the last day in the house, I am sick, feverish, storm outside, love this place, I am here, the last day, do not stop thinking of it, it was not me in the quilt, sunk into the couch, I did not know how to sail yet, did not know the sea, had never seen the beach, the cove, Hannah was not going to be married and live in England, Gramma was alive, I had no homework, it was not me on this couch, did not know what beating off was, I think I knew what making love was then, we learned in fifth grade, did I know when I was in the quilt on the couch, fifth grade only just started, maybe I knew something of it, embarrassed by the part about pubic hair, probably only had a first inkling of what making love was, looking at Hannah and Dan, always doing homework, imagined they knew what everything was, did not want to learn, they always across the room under the lamp studying, I always in quilt, feverish, it was not me that was there, I am not who was there, it is me here now, I keep changing, keep nothing, should I keep anything, keep only what I want, can, not this house, this place, I am not Simmy as I was, do love my childhood, do not love anything since Gramma died, cannot make any love, on the edge of childhood now still, only ready to teach sixth grade, never think back to this place, flood it over, vague memories, do not want to keep changing, I keep changing, if I wanted to keep changing I would decide to change, decide, then change, hold on to things, make Dan listen to me, what I want to say, not shut up and listen to him, must talk to Dan my way, mad at him, had enough of this silence, organ, monk, I have sat here thinking slowly, thought nothing, Dan must have thought much more, will talk to him, not quite, he is asleep, what do I think of, shadow at my window, keep thinking of that, shadow at my window, alone in my bed, wind in the woods, somehow a shadow at the window, bear from the woods, lie in the bed knowing the bear is there, just on the other side of the screen of my window, came out of the woods, breathing huffily, can hear him, he smells me inside, I lie there knowing he is there, the bear is there, I keep thinking of it, do not want to be myself when I was a child, DAN, ARE YOU AWAKE?

Dan's Thoughts

My secret games, didn't want anyone to see my lists, could I explain lists like that, could I explain Biography of Timothy Usk, justify time spent on it, spent most of my time making such things, drawers full of them, made-up histories, biographies, programs for concerts, how Usk learned his music as a boy from a few old seventy-eights in Alaska where he was born, the Pathétique Sonata, the Pastoral Symphony, all those pieces I first knew myself, his old Auntie played piano in the saloon, taught Tim to play after his Pa was dead, wild old man, had lived in cabin on outskirts of Nome, somewhat of a madman, a blacksmith, a trapper, had old Victrola brought on dogsled from Anchorage, had old sets of seventy-eights, had miniature study scores such as Uncle Jake collected, works of Beethoven, Mozart, Brahms, Pa used to follow scores along with his records, had once been a musician, escaped off to Alaska when he went mad, took young wife who played violin, but she put it away in closet in their cabin, never played it, cold, lonely, hopeless place, Auntie sang bawdy songs for old coots hanging around saloon, even played a little Mozart sonata, taught Tim something about piano, then he taught himself, taught himself by listening and fiddling around with Ma's violin too and looking at Pa's miniature scores, they were put away in closet too after Pa shot himself when Tim was five, Tim didn't remember his pa except as drunk old man, would smash records in a fit, not all, enough left to learn from, sometimes one of a set would be missing, Tim only knew two records of Mozart's Thirty-eighth, third record smashed by Pa in drunken fit, Tim imagined missing sides for himself, that started him composing in his mind, made up missing parts of Mozart, later got so he could figure out scores, how they were written, could see how parts that had gotten smashed went, sang them to himself, Tim figured out just by listening how to write it down, from the records wrote down a whole Beethoven quartet, wrote a quartet of his own, had no idea how it would sound except in his head, mostly wrote little pieces he could play on Auntie's piano in saloon after hours, that was late at night, or he'd get up early and play, disturbed the sleep of some of the whores, whores were nice to him though, a strange sort of childhood, didn't know other kids his age, not many of them in Nome, busy composing Mozart and Beethoven and his own pieces, kids didn't understand him, Auntie was a whore herself, maybe she wasn't Pa's actual sister, but Pa ended up in Nome because of her, she'd been there for years,

he followed her, Ma was frail, Ma loved Pa somehow, Ma and
Auntie great pals, Ma would've gone on playing violin but
didn't have heart for it the worse Pa got, the wilder he got,
chasing her about with shotgun sometimes, smashing old
seventy-eights, big dark man, Ma worked as barmaid, after
he shot himself she got frailer and frailer, Auntie took care
of Tim mostly, or whores did, they did like Tim, Ma didn't
want him taking her violin from closet, didn't want to hear
it, would cry when she heard him play, not a madman at all
like his Pa, but classical, pure, restrained, he'd never heard
any music less classical than Brahms, only a few bawdy
songs of Auntie's and strange Eskimo music, he'd go listen
to Eskimos when they passed through town, didn't talk to
them, wrote down some of their odd tunes, their Asian eyes
watching him while they pounded fish, Tim didn't know
what they were singing, never really went to school, Ma
taught him to read at home, never cared about much but
music, liked to stay out in cold alone, long walks when no
one else would stay out, watched the frozen strait, played
piano in the cold saloon when they kept the fire low because
there weren't any customers, what do I know about Nome, I
don't know a thing, I can make it all up, I put him there in
my mind, he couldn't be from here, had to be far away and
odd and alone, entirely in the cold, I own a square inch of
land up there myself, always my secret home, the land I
own, I put him there, I became Timothy Usk when I mowed
lawns, dripping hot summer, mower would make awful
noise, up and down I'd go, our yard, neighbors' yards, I'd sing
to myself under noise, I was Tim Usk walking along the
cold sea, imagining his new quartet, his new sonata, a little
violin concerto for his Ma, he didn't know she'd been dying,
Auntie knew that, when she died Auntie took Tim in, room

behind the bar, sometimes slept upstairs with whores, was an innocent sort of boy, didn't know any girls his own age, don't know what whores did with him, if they used him for things they might enjoy, if they just kept him comfortable and warm, if he first made love when he was only a kid and his Ma had just died, or if he never made love with a whore, do know some things about his troubles later down in Seattle when he was sent off by the whores who saved the money for him to go, Auntie made them understand what a genius Tim might be, she knew he was because she'd been in the south, Auntie was fat, no one cared for her, she could be bawdy when she wanted to, she got people to listen to her and laugh along, all Tim did was compose, composed to remember his Ma, composed his first big work, piano sonata like the Pathétique, didn't know what Pathétique meant, made it sound like himself, like nothing else he'd heard, Uskian, I began to recognize it, how can I explain it, how can I explain his music to myself, it didn't express itself extremely, must look closely for its expressiveness, clear music, a paring down, partly because he didn't have much paper, had to draw staves himself, wrote very small to get enough on a page, small as miniature scores, only kind he knew, his eyes were bad, he'd hunch over piano in bad light of cold saloon, his fingers too numb to play complicatedly, never music to show off, only cared about tune and what he could do with it, barest subtlest of harmonic changes, rhythmic changes, why such a classicist, why mowing lawns did I hear such pure music, why didn't I huff and puff and explode romantically, must have left that to Mahler, wrote down Usk's themes, thematic catalogue of his works, he wrote music all the time, living with Auntie in whorehouse, in saloon, lonely sad years taken care of by whores, no real friends, wrote quartets and sonatas, then just before he was sent off to Seattle wrote the Variations Without A Theme, tune kept changing, no starting point, no ending, was how Tim felt about himself, drifting, scared because he was older now, Auntie wanted to send him south, didn't know himself yet or his music, what it could become, didn't want to go, she'd cry over how bad she felt, he being a genius and she not able to give him enough, thought he should get away to real music, learn what she could never teach, save himself from only knowing whores and old coots at the saloon, told him there were kids like him down south in Seattle, kids who played pianos and violins and listened to music all the time, even kids who composed it like he did, a school of them, there was printed-up paper he could buy with staves already on it, and bigger so it wouldn't hurt his eyes, and much more beautiful-sounding pianos, whole orchestras, Tim didn't want to go, afraid it'd be too warm, afraid of what people would be like, liked the old whores, they were enough, was a big fellow, framed like his Pa, tall, sturdy, bit of a beard, whores liked him, never wrote letters to them from Seattle, only to Auntie who'd read them to all the whores too, the whole houseful of women missing him after they'd convinced him to go, his leaving sad for all of them, they'd put their money together, put him on truck for Anchorage, coastal steamer from there, going back down the way his father had come up, took his music in a big duffel, took all the clothes he had, wrote Auntie all the time from Seattle at first, put up in rooming house, lonely, afraid, first lecture he went to was terrified by some new music, wasn't really new, just Wagner, old and familiar to most, Tim left room, afraid the southern world had different music, didn't hear things he heard, walked about in fear, heard all the noises of all the instruments from practice rooms, much more real sounding than on old seventy-eights, but more terrifying, went to first piano lesson, played Pathétique, teacher overwhelmed, asked him to play again, called in other teachers, asked to play something else, played his own Variations, teachers had never heard music like it, not modern music but not old either, didn't sound like anything any of them had heard, can't explain it to myself, experienced only at moments in lawn mowing, with motor roaring loud and sweat dripping all over me, down chest and into shorts and down legs, sun in eyes and couldn't see or feel or hear anything but music in my head, Uskian moments, music I would dream about, music never heard before, imagined how Tim would compose all the time, his scores were tidy, not tortured, not full of second thoughts, worked slowly, logically, never spoke of work, Tim didn't understand other students, didn't like them because they were so clever, he stayed alone, went to a whorehouse when he found where one was, but wasn't like home for him, wanted to go home for summer, which he did, when Auntie greeted him he cried for whole evening, played her new pieces as best he could on saloon piano, his music somewhat different now, was reacting to things down there, had heard enough of that modern music to make him very mad, didn't want to hear it, wanted to write his own, but had also heard things he hadn't suspected, he had only known middle quartets minus a few smashed sides, hadn't known what Beethoven wrote next, his old Beethoven friend began to scare him, there was much more of him, unexpected things, hard to understand, all in different directions from what Tim might have imagined, didn't make as much sense anymore, and suddenly there were four

Brahms symphonies instead of two, suddenly there was this
Wagner, there was this Mahler who terrified him most,
more terrifying than all the rest of modern music, and just
as surprising and sudden there were lightweight unbreakable records, had all the music on two sides instead of
twelve, clearer, each instrument more itself than before,
now Tim would stand outside practice rooms for hours
listening to different sounds of instruments, tried to play
them, played viola in string quartet, never got to be friends
with other members, they just needed a viola, didn't like
him much, found him strange, never got far with wind
instruments, couldn't control his breath, very short of
breath, breathed better up in Alaska, relaxed more too, felt
at home there in summer, told Auntie he didn't like city,
didn't like heat, found all the people cruel, said whores
there weren't the same, they treated you coldly, found no
girls his own age who were friendly to him, kept to himself,
his rooming house, his lessons, gave a recital now and then,
his teacher promised that if he wrote a symphony it would
be played next year by student orchestra, was hard at work
all summer, got nowhere, spent some time with Eskimos
too when they came into town, would sit and listen to
them, watch them, write down their tunes, wonder where
Eskimos had come from, why only they were left of all the
tribes that had come across and gone south, how whole
continent had been peopled by way of the frozen strait, how
Nome was farthest reach of white people to the west and
also bridge for yellow people to the east, where were those
white people from and where were those yellow people
from, both from steppes of central Asia, other side of world
from here, this is my own thinking now not Tim Usk's, how
it said in our new atlas on historical map of migrations a

paragraph printed in blankish space where Tannu Tuva used to be that here was the source of nomads spreading westward into Europe, and now I imagine from this same source came and passed people even earlier going other way, crossing the strait, pouring down into America out of that far valley, all the same people, same source, first east, then west, and finally the descendants of westward-faring Tannu Tuva crossed an ocean, pressed as far west as Nome, and the descendants of eastward-faring Tannu Tuva crossed the strait and funneled into whole continent, set up camp on this riverbank here in Illinois, and those from east and those from west met here for first time in centuries since they had left their desert fountain, fought battle even perhaps in our own meadow, Gramma's meadow, we've found arrowheads, bones, burial mound deep in woods, and my Gramma has retold story of these wars word for word to her club, pretending she had written it herself, and I read her telling of it and the books too, how here in this valley the world came full circle and Black Hawk was defeated and banished beyond Mississippi, dying looking back across into Illinois, the lost homeland, he and his nation seeping into earth, drying up, as the source Tannu Tuva had by then run dry too, once the fountain of great barbarous hordes, now almost unpeopled, flutes calling over empty valleys, a land I dreamed, keeping my mind busy, returning to, lonely, cold, stories that grew from childhood, chosen because of its lovely name, Ma read me names of countries of the world, Oubangui-Chari, Ruanda-Urundi, Tannu Tuva, I liked it best, home of all my animals, a whole history of imagined kings, and then in time I became realistic, animals banished to closet, now a land of people, imagined dusty towns by the Yenisey River with towers and back alleys and roads

leading out, map showed Tannu Tuva so small, had to draw
bigger maps myself, filled in the emptiness, roads, railroads,
towns, far valleys, nowhere I could read anything about
Tannu Tuva, never much known, quite forgotten once over-
run by Stalin, what are sixty thousand shepherds in world's
vastness, I invented them, made at times marvelous de-
mocracies with enlightened citizenry, other times colorful
despots and oppressed peasants, made their music, Hannah
and I, playing ocarinas and banging potato chip cans into
microphone, replaying tape at slower speed, ocarinas became moans of horns across valleys, cans became thunder
drums, slow, processional, grand movements of coronation
march, dance of village chieftain, Hannah tootled soprano
ocarina for shepherd flutes, still have tapes, hidden in bottom of drawer, in music I hear landscapes always, stormy
Mahler and these woods, simple clear Usk and his frozen
strait, drums and horns of Tannu Tuva, might I ever go
there, rather not ever see it, depressing gray corrugated
prefab Soviet structures, no tents of sheepskin, no clay
towns, no ornamentation of doorways and archways, elabo-
rate Tannu Tuvan designs such as I once imagined, drunk-
enness on festival days when king processes through city,
drums and dances, I lying on stomach alongside trickle in
bottom of gully, looking sideways, head on elbow, imagining stormy festival within walls of dirt, drumbeats, shepherds from surrounding country into city for drunken
week, I might stay out in gully even till sunset to watch
light change in made-up land, see tiny shadows lengthen,
lie so flat against bottom of gully I could look up and see
sunset colors behind my towers, almost see dust of desert
rising around my city as shepherd might see it from a far
valley, only barely hear drums and bells and horns carried

on wind, driving the king's limousine along my roads, stopping at villages for cheers of people in desert robes, king
going to country palace, a castle such as my Gramma's,
miniature of it, woods around it of moss and weeds, tower
peeking out of them, is Sim up there on edge playing with
monkeys, wanted once to see sun rise over my towers, never
could get up early enough, imagined music of sunrise,
drums and bells waking up towns, on our tape we made
sunrise ceremony, Ma's glass dessert bowls for bells, Tannu
Tuvan orchestra of horns and drums and flutes and bells,
anthropological field recordings, documented all that, files
on Tannu Tuva, lists, useless to anyone else, how could I
justify time spent on it, could I explain lists like those, what
if someone had seen my list of complete works of Timothy
Usk, you mean all these timings say how long this movement is and how long that movement is, why do you do this,
why don't you learn actually to write these pieces of music
that don't exist, never wrote more than the themes so I
could remember them, I did put an end to Timothy Usk at a
certain age, Tim had hard times, terrible tortured times,
Auntie encouraged him to return south, didn't want to go,
whores disappointed if he didn't, went for their sake, for
their caring of him, missed them, wrote Auntie still all the
time, perhaps this time at last a woman came into his life,
another student, cellist, wrote a quintet with extra cello so
she could play with his string quartet, he liked her very
much, perhaps they made love, she stayed with him
through performance of quintet, some small fame, taped for
radio, chosen for new recording of promising young composers, by this time cellist had had it with him, end of
whatever there might have been, his long letters to Auntie
told nothing of this cellist, had Tim ever truly known her,

had he only imagined her for what she might have been for him, what little practice he'd had at knowing people, knew no one, never expected to, knew things only in musical language, could hardly speak, seemed slow-witted, dull, big sturdy fellow by then, beard, messy, smelled bad, belonged up in Alaska, put all tidiness into music, music became clearer still, at turn of year he suddenly panicked, longed for snows of north, wet dreariness of Seattle driving him mad, cellist tormenting his loneliness, who knows what she herself really was, whores in south no good, no friends, his teacher finding him difficult, impatient with him, Tim not as impressionable as teacher had hoped, more than all these difficulties was shock of discovering music in its vastness, only known before in single instances like Pathétique and Pastoral, now music burst out of the plastic unbreakable records turning slowly on these marvelous machines, no more breaks in music to turn record over which had accounted for those curious pauses every five minutes or so in Usk's earlier scores, no more fear of breaking the only documents, the only teachers, no more frantic whirling of the fragile disc on crackly faint old Victrola, now music everywhere, libraries full of full-size scores, real instruments tootling and sawing away about him, pianos such as he'd never imagined pianos could be, no missing keys, no fuzzy notes, and more than all the new music on thousands of records it was the surprisingness of the explorations his familiar Beethoven had made without him, he felt he must explore too, if he had lived longer and had time to get used to things slowly Tim might have come to understand the progression, but that Mahler, he took too long, was too loud, needed too many instruments, tried to overwhelm him, he walked out of concert when Mahler was played, went to

look again at what his friend Beethoven had done after
middle quartets, puzzled for weeks, felt betrayed first, but
drawn back, kept puzzling, felt could learn nothing of it all
in Seattle, they could never make him understand, decided
to run, told no one, would go home, packed scores of puzzling quartets in his duffel, all the clothes he had, stacks of
printed music paper, new pair of thick glasses to help him
see, might be going blind, left his room in dark night, no
messages for anyone, waited at dock for steamer, early
spring, sailed up coast with its mountains to Anchorage,
found a northern whore for a night, began to feel home
again, got the weekly truck to Nome, whores worried, Auntie had had no word of him for weeks, he didn't write as
much anymore, he walked right into saloon with duffel on
his back, shouts of welcome, worried questions, old coots
turned slowly around, eyed him foggily, never liked young
Tim, no one liked him in town except whores, too odd for
everyone, odder than Pa, Auntie gave him room again in
back of bar, he slept during days, as summer came sun hurt
his eyes more, sun shining late into evenings, he stayed
inside, took walks only at midnight when sun quite low on
horizon, came back to find saloon quiet, coots staggered
home, couple of whores still with customers, Auntie
snoring behind her door, he'd very quietly pick things out
on piano, its tuning bothered him now, its tone, came to
write much of his music in his head, directly onto paper,
would write at poker table under dim lamp all night long,
good thing he had full-size music paper, even so had to get
quite close to it, wrote notes bigger and bigger, many sheets
of paper, wrote very slowly, had come to feel he had written
too much music, decided to slow down, concentrate, felt he
had little time, couldn't imagine living his life in that

saloon for too long, wondered if he was sick, felt he didn't
care, knew he was dying of his own accord, sensed his own
time going, wanted it to, music now puzzled him, not joy,
not thing to delight in, not tidy, not clear, but tortured and
difficult, didn't come to him at once, had to rework, scratch
out staves, pages, manuscripts now nearly indecipherable,
became more so as he went blind, that summer worked
again on symphony, a plunge into intense feeling for his
youth, back to it, wiped out teachers and students, returned
to music itself inside him as he felt it, full of sadness,
fragmented tunes, angular, rough, so much to explore, written at height of summer, midnight sun, brightness, would
see no such brightness again, darkness would come, would
die in dark winter which even then began to come on,
exhausted by symphony, couldn't work for a month, spoke
little, played nothing for Auntie, didn't sleep with whores,
they were older, fatter, there were four of them besides
Auntie, a favorite old one had died, Auntie not well herself,
Tim colder to her, she was not as she had been, didn't
understand his return, perhaps didn't want him back,
wanted him off making his name in world, had thought too
much of his genius, not for his sake, perhaps only for what it
meant to her, had she ever loved his music, or only been
proud, Tim came to resent her at times, would not talk with
her, scowled, turned shoulder, retreated to room, slept a
good deal, often kept eyes closed, then as real coldness
edged in took himself to outskirts of town, unboarded Pa's
cabin, set himself up there, Auntie glad to see him go, he
spent time chopping wood for winter, already quite cold,
began a new piece, Quadruple Concerto, his tour de force,
piano, violin, viola, cello, and whole orchestra as well, all
mixing in and out of themselves in revolving patterns, noth-

ing holding to itself, constant changes, four instruments in spontaneous conversation, Tim's way of talking, he had now ceased actual talking, once or twice a word when going to town for provisions, but weeks of silence, never going to see Auntie, never the whores, as darkness came on so did silence, no more went to play piano in saloon, played only in head the perfect pianos of the south, heard sounds even they did not make, his rickety kitchen table worn at the edge by his pounding on it as if it were keyboard, what silent recitals he had in his cold cabin in darkening winter, heard Quadruple Concerto forming itself on paper, let four instruments talk, did not talk himself, they told it, he discovered them, frost closing in his cabin, sensed he would not emerge, did something he would not have done before in music, composed the gunshot of his father's death, one stroke, unmusical, remembering the shot sounding in the other room in the cold night, felt it might have been Pa hammering at the forge, hammer stroke on anvil, but Pa shot self in head, now Tim opened again the forge next to the cabin, made that stroke on the anvil with Pa's hammer, the old sound, added to his score the stroke of the hammer, only he knew what it signified, Tim had nightmares daily when he slept, snow had begun, nothing to be seen out his frosty windows but deeper whiteness, depths of snow, and that only for a time at midday, as it drew on to darkest day of year the swirl of white could only be sensed, swirl was in darkness, lone cabin all alone in darkness, he hardly seeing, seeing only enough to scribble the big notes, was gaunt now, didn't eat much, only to keep barely living, ended his concerto in terrible darkness, refused to spend Christmas with Auntie and whores, wouldn't let her in as she pounded outside on his door, she in fright, guilty, screaming, trembling for days, took cold, near to death herself but brought round again after turn of year, now angry at Tim, vowed not to see him, losing mind somewhat, she threatened to burn old scores he'd left in saloon, his sonatas, quartets, the quintet, everything, whores had to stop her more than once, snapped out of that madness finally but left a bleak woman, depressed, never took a customer again, stared blankly, meanwhile Tim in cabin on outskirts of town, saw no one ever again, spoke no word, wrote one piece more, his mind clear again after these dreams, with so little to eat, so much cold, concentrated on mental work, Variations on Two Themes, an Eskimo fish-pounding tune and a bawdy song, themes he'd long remembered, now to explore them, logical, clear, to show how he'd come through and he knew things, could face death and still work, then the page faded before him, could no longer see notes, if last page is decipherable it will take much scholarly work, and after he penned it, sometime in deep winter, so he wouldn't merely starve, so he need never talk again, he walked out in snow, north, away from town, stumbled in snow and let it keep falling on him, his frozen skinny body not found till thaw, his empty cabin approached by town authorities at whores' request, his last three pieces found stacked on rickety worn-edged kitchen table with message that these were his only pieces, had written them in order to put down everything he knew, now let me die, in spring the whores saw the frozen body buried, Auntie was now a giggly old lady who made no sense, whores sent three final works and all other manuscripts they had saved from Auntie's rage down to his teacher, they were performed in Seattle, then elsewhere, the three final works, performed many times, we all know how in few years since death the name of Timothy

Usk has become known, his complete works published and recorded and sent to the corners of the world wherever Western music is played, where there are LP record players, WHAT DID YOU SAY?

Conversation
(Sim, Dan)

Hang over the railing, Dan, look down. I used to be afraid of climbing the tower. I was always afraid of heights. I'm still a little afraid. Did Uncle Toby paint that compass on the floor?

I suppose it was Uncle Toby, the swirls and little leaves, north, south, east, west. Gramma didn't like all those twisty swirls Uncle Toby kept making everywhere on her floors and ceilings and over her doors.

It's begun to fade. I used to be afraid to climb these stairs, and I was afraid of having to pass that gnome carved on the banister on the next landing.

There he is. He was meant to be friendly with his hand out to shake yours. Hannah and I used to shake his hand and tell him not to let any capitalists up. I hope Uncle Toby's murals are still in the tower room. I wouldn't be surprised if the monks had painted them over. No, they're here, look. They've faded a lot too. We're all in them. Do you remember where he put you in?

Me in?

He put in our faces when we were kids. Whenever we got to be about six, he'd paint us in as little gnomes. I know exactly where I am, there under the window. You can hardly tell it's me. There must've been a leak here. They've had to replaster in places. There's Hannah with her glasses by the chimney, a curly-haired little gnome. There you are, I think, under that tree.

That's supposed to be me?

Everything's faded so much. You can't tell who everyone is. We'll ask Uncle Toby what it's all supposed to be. I don't remember my Norse gods very well. He put the family's faces on the gods. That's our Grandfather with the ravens, Wotan, I guess. That's Gramma on the chariot pulled by sheep. The sheep have faded right into the plaster. I think Pa was in the part that's plastered over. There must've been a leak above that window. I think that's Ma's hand holding the rope and her other hand holding the shears. You can't see her face, it's all faded. Those big blankish spaces were the legs of giants, just the legs, floor to ceiling, you had to imagine the rest of them. That's Uncle Toby, the big gnome climbing up the wall along the stairs. It was always moist and leaky up here. The paint was fading from the sun even back then. We'd sit up here on these swinging couches, swinging back and forth, Hannah and me, planning secret missions. Familiar rusty sound of the chains.

You can see the road almost straight below over the bluff, Dan. I can see the gargoyles.

They're waterspouts from the gutters. Uncle Toby made cement gargoyles around the spouts. What was he like when he was doing all this? He wasn't much older than I am now. It's hard to think back before we were born, to think of Pa and Tommy and Maddy being kids here, and Jake. We'll get some stories from Uncle Toby. Pa never talks about it. He said he would never come back here.

You can really see from here, Dan, how it's all plain old farm buildings and we're in the silo.

And the library's the corncrib. Look, Sim, there's a monk walking through the arch. What can they possibly do all day long? Down there in the courtyard was my favorite place to sit, except for the bees. The arches on either side, the sunken garden, the crenellations on the garage roof where Hannah and I would spy for capitalists. I remember Pa skimming squishy little crab apples out of the wading pool with a net, wrinkled and shriveled like newborn babies' heads.

We'd play our army games up there on the roof too, shooting out from behind.

I remember Aunt Maddy sitting in the courtyard with her little Toby, and before that, when she was the age I am now, when she wasn't married yet. She was back here at home staying around. I don't think Gramma understood what her problems were. Gramma'd expected her to be married by then.

Look over here, Dan. The big swimming pool looks strange with snow in it, a snow crater. That must be how your Tannu Tuva looks now, out in the meadow. You sure you don't want to go look at it?

And see, Sim, if you look down the lane of pines there at the end of the pool, you can see, sort of, the circle in the woods, that lighter space there. I dream so often of flying out this window, sailing out over the pool, diving into the grass in the middle of the circle, or swinging off this tower on a huge chain that I can swing on way out over everything, the pool, the woods, the bluff, all sorts of dreams of sailing through the air. And it makes me think of how when Hannah and I were small, Edna would walk with us down the lane to the circle of trees and to the lookout. That was when we could walk only as fast as she could. She was more crotchety and kept her hair all blued by the time you came along. Edna was in Uncle Toby's mural too. She was over there, I think, where it's been replastered. She was a ghastly-looking creature stuck up to her waist in the ground. She never knew about the murals because she couldn't climb the stairs on her short bowlegs. She never got above the first floor.

I was afraid of Edna. She was short and round, and I was afraid of her feet. They'd grown funny. She showed me once how the toes overlapped.

She loved scaring us with stories of Staleen. She'd tell us how he'd send people to the depths of Siberia where they froze to death working on chain gangs in the snow. She said we'd be sent to Siberia if we ever went over there, if Staleen ever caught Americans he'd send them to freeze to death. I decided I wanted to go there, of course. That's why I made up Tannu Tuva, not to let myself get frightened by her stories. Don't push so hard, Sim, let it swing just a bit, glide. This is the rhythm I remember, back and forth, sitting here with Hannah. I probably dream the feeling of flying out this window from having swung on this couch so much. See that trapdoor up there for putting the flag on the tower? Uncle Jake would climb up in the old days. Hannah and I once had a great Bulganin and Khrushchev plan to put our hammer and sickle flag up there. We knew we wouldn't actually do it, but it was a plan we worked out, how we'd get a ladder, attach the flag, when we'd do it, our secret communist revolution. We'd get in the closet at home and hide in the coats, and I'd put one end of the vacuum cleaner hose up

the sleeve of the coat I was in, and Hannah'd put the other
end up the sleeve of the coat she was in, and we'd whisper
B and K plans. Hey, Hannah! Workers of the world, unite!
Hey, Dan! You have nothing to lose but your chains! I remember Ma saying: How did we get children like this!

There are so many things you and Hannah did.

I wish you'd do some talking, Sim. I keep telling you
things I did. I'd rather listen to you. I should shut up.

I like hearing your things now. It's not the way it used
to be.

But you should tell me things. I want to hear you talk.
Whatever you want to say, not what I ask you. It's hard
for me to shut up, but I will, I want to. Tell me something.

I used to think there were bears in the woods as I was
falling asleep alone. You know how I always slept in the
room below the library with the window at ground level
looking out at the woods? I was remembering that. I had a
hard time getting to sleep when I was small out here. I never
told Ma I was afraid. She'd leave the hall light on and the
door open a crack, and there'd always be a rectangle of light
on the wall opposite the bed.

Didn't you tell anyone?

I knew there weren't any bears there, there was nothing
to be afraid of. But at the same time I couldn't get to sleep.

You do remember things, Sim, about being here.

I remember some few things. I was trying to think of
them when we were in the library. I was trying to remember
Gramma. I seem to remember her poking me when she
went swimming with us in the pool. I remember the skirt of
her bathing suit fluttering in the water. I remember when I
left Dotted-Swiss outdoors all night. Do you remember
about the bear who is there?

The bear?

One of the things I used to say. I used to call Dotted-Swiss the bear who is there. I'd say: Where is the bear who is there? And you'd have to answer: Here is the bear who is there. You don't remember that?

It must've been something you did with Hannah and Ma.

I remember the way I'd say it, the rhythm: WHERE is the BEAR who is THERE? Do you want to know something?

What?

I was thinking about this in the library.

What?

A thought I've always had, thinking I was an after-thought, not just an afterthought, actually a mistake. They didn't want another kid. They didn't want another Tannu Tuvan leaping about the place. I'll bet you never thought of that before.

You think of yourself as an afterthought?

I always have. As a mistake.

I don't think you were a mistake.

How did they explain it to you, Dan, when I was coming along?

They told us, Ma did, that we were getting a new member of the family. It sounded like they'd planned you, but she couldn't say if you would be a brother or a sister. It was as if she knew, but it was a secret from Hannah and me.

Which did you want?

I did want a brother, but I felt odd beforehand, sort of imagined him as a brother about my size, though I knew perfectly well you'd be a baby, but I imagined you somehow as about my size, so it was odd when you were so small.

How did Hannah feel?

We weren't upset about you. We were jealous of each

other, who got to hold you the most, for a while, then we went back to playing our own games.

You know what I was thinking in the library? I wanted to talk to you the way I think, not the way we were talking before, not the way you keep talking, Dan, explaining things, but talk to you the way I think, see if you'd listen, understand it, though it's confusing, not thinking straight, not organizing things.

Talk that way, Sim. Please, Sim, keep talking, go on.

I don't know. I felt for a minute I could talk to you the way I think.

All right.

All right, listen, this is what I mean. I can't remember things. I remember facts. I don't remember things that happened. I can't remember if Gramma poked me or not. I can remember some things, like the rectangle of light on the wall when I went to sleep, and the shadow of the bear at the window.

The bear who is there?

I keep thinking of it. These are things I'm trying to remember back before I can remember, remembering the feeling of playing in the grass with the plastic monkeys. I haven't remembered it. Or in the bed cuddling up with Dotted-Swiss. She was the bear who is there. The bear at the window was the bear who isn't there. I think that was it. Do you remember anything like that? I'm trying to remember for the first time. You've kept those things in your mind all along. You've kept your files full of them. I forgot them all when we moved. I forgot all the things I'd done for ten years. I haven't thought of them. So that even coming back here doesn't mean anything to me because it's not familiar. I don't remember what it felt like being here. I don't have those feelings in me. I can't feel them anymore. You know exactly what it was like because you remember it. You recognize the coat of arms and the moldings and these murals. I don't remember these things. I remember lights and shadows to an extent, the feeling of being poked, maybe, and splashing in the pool, peeking out with our guns from the garage roof, maybe the baby in the courtyard, little Toby, I can't remember. I try to remember the feeling of playing with the plastic monkeys, watching them move. That's what interested me. I didn't expect to keep them. They got thrown out. I don't have them in my closet. I gave them all up when we moved. All things changed before my eyes. I never expected them not to. My sailboat is the finest place for me. The wind always moves, the water always moves. That's why I like to play sports. The play is always moving, the ball lands in an unpredictable spot, you are in an unpredictable spot. It doesn't matter if there are rules and teams. I forget them. I like the moving.

Good, Sim, keep talking your way. I like it.

How do I talk my way? That's why I don't talk much. The way I am can't be talked. I should be a monk with a vow of silence. I don't want to be that way. I fight being a watcher. I would always be a watcher if I didn't fight it. I would sit in a meadow and watch birds fly up and bugs crawl and smell the smells, that's all I would need to do. I would sleep a lot. I wouldn't have to do anything. I force myself to do what I'm afraid of. I forced myself to play sports. I wouldn't have played sports, I wouldn't have gone sailing. I would've sat, slept. What makes people do things? I never wanted to do anything with anybody. I dreaded coming out here because I knew we'd have to play army games, and what other games Jake would want to play.

You know, Sim, I always used to think when I was small that of course I would have to go in the army. I always feared it. Edna used to say: Oh, Danny, I pray every night that the Lord won't let there be no war when you're in the army. I pray that old Staleen won't make no trouble for my poor Danny when he's in the army. I remember her talking on the phone with one of her friends, someone else's cook from down the street, about how they dropped another bum, she called it the bum, another test of the bum, oh Lord, ain't the world awful! Oh, Danny, I just pray there ain't no war when you grow up! All the talk about oh Lord, the bum, and old Staleen. Hannah and I had to listen to that day after day. Go on talking, Sim. I interrupted you.

I want to talk about something else, about what I was saying about the sources of love.

All right.

I want to tell you what I mean about it. You don't understand. This goes way back. That's what I was thinking down in the library. All right, I won't think about it. Let me see. No one loved me. No one loved me. I only felt the bear did, or else it was me loving myself, or I could love it a way I wanted someone to love me. I'm explaining too much. But there were the two bears, Dotted-Swiss and then the other one who wasn't there, only the shadow. I was afraid of it. I wasn't afraid of anything else. I'm trying to say I was always afraid of one thing, not sailing and sports and army games, but all one thing. It was always there. I always sensed it, with claws, a shadow at the window. No, I'll stop explaining it. The whole business is that I was expected to go to sleep by myself and not be afraid. What a grown-up he is, they'd say. I was treated as much more grown up because I was the afterthought, been through this already, but I was very

afraid, and I was expected to go to sleep by myself, and I
pretended I could, never to go to sleep with anyone, never to
have anyone to sleep with. You want to know where I first
made love. That can happen anywhere. Where did you first
make love? Out in the grass there beyond the pool. I did it
somewhere else, but where did you first sleep with someone? I don't mean fall asleep together. I mean sleep, settled
in with each other, trusting, allowing you to sleep, holding
each other or maybe not even that, just sleep. I had Dotted-
Swiss to sleep with. I needed her to sleep with until I was in
high school. I pretended she was just an extra pillow, but I
had to sleep with her or I couldn't sleep. Everyone else was
older. Soon Hannah was married and went off to England
and you were with Mir. I was the only one who didn't sleep
with anyone. Ma and Pa made it so I never would. I still have
not. That's what you don't understand. You're curious about
the facts. What I don't understand is the things I can't say,
why I don't listen to music. I don't understand it, don't care.
I don't understand how you talk about the feelings of it,
how you talk about politics, why you care. I don't even
understand how you talk about Mir. You feel something.
Where does it come from? Who gave it to you? I don't have
the feeling. Do you know that everyone I knew always got
up and left, walked home, got up and left. You can't imagine
it. I'm quiet and don't have feelings. Only wishes. Can
wishes be feelings? They don't exist yet. You can't have
feelings if you haven't had them yet. Wishes are things you
haven't had. Why do I trust you now, Dan? I never trusted
you before. You're the person in the world I trust, the person
who can make me feel better by talking. Maybe it's that
you're different from me and it doesn't matter. I don't want
you to be the same as me. It's that you're here and talk to

me, even though I did get mad because you talk on and explain things. I'm making no sense. Someone listening to me would think I was very confused.

I'm confused. It doesn't matter, Sim. I understand some of it.

Whenever I've spent the night with someone I've not been able to sleep. I have a terrible nervous restless night. I've never slept with someone more than one night in a row. I'm too tired, I can't. Ma and Pa wanted me always to sleep alone. As far as they know I never slept with anyone. They're secretly relieved by it.

But they didn't want me to sleep with anyone either. They didn't want Mir, or anyone else.

But you did, but you did, and they knew about it. With me they don't know about anyone, never have, no names. Neither do you, just assuming. Doesn't it puzzle you? Who do you think I could've ever slept with?

Why do you think I asked you about it before? I want to find out these things. I don't know your secrets. I won't shake them out, as long as you know you can tell me if you want. Do you want Ma and Pa to want to know?

I don't expect it.

But you want it.

You want them to change. I don't expect it. Why want it?

Don't you expect anything from them, Sim? I expect too much. I'm a perfectionist. That's what Pa said to me. He gave me a long talk about my perfectionism a couple of days before Christmas when I was there, before you got down. I didn't tell you about it. I wouldn't have told you then. We hadn't talked to each other much yet, had we?

What did he tell you?

My idea was to tell him, tell them both, Ma too, she kept

going back and forth to the kitchen baking cookies, kept coming back and saying: What did I miss, what did I miss? My idea was to tell them that Mir and I wouldn't be living together after the turn of the year. I felt I owed them a discussion of it. I'd not discussed it with them for years because I knew they didn't like us living together. That's why I wanted to talk to them, to keep them from gloating privately over it, feeling they'd won at last. It wasn't that I owed them a discussion. I wanted to explain exactly what had happened, so they'd not be able to take comfort in it. They had to understand it as a defeat for them. They always felt she took advantage of me. I supported her through school and what I worked at hadn't been anything I might eventually make my life of. When they gave me presents of money, you know, it was earmarked. Danny, just spend this on yourself, clothes, books, whatever you want. We just don't want it going for rent. You have to buy things for yourself. I told them I had enough clothes, I could only read a certain number of books, I didn't want to be going on trips. They didn't understand why I didn't want a better job by now. I told them I liked easygoing jobs, I didn't need much money, free time was what I wanted. They don't understand that it didn't matter that I paid for things while Mir went to school. She needed it, I didn't, for what we'd each chosen to do. That wasn't our problem. It was the love between us that wasn't making it work. And I told them, so they would know it was the lack of love that made it not work. Not Mir's lack, but my lack. I couldn't find myself able to love her certainly. She was also uncertain. It's not all my doing. But to me it was important that Ma and Pa see I had not been able to live with Mir. I myself had not been able to. That was my defeat and theirs, not hers. She may have been defeated too, but that wasn't their business. When I went down there to tell them all this, Pa said I must have some idea I'd find this ever-running fount of love. And he said of course it didn't exist, and I said of course it didn't. I wasn't talking about such a thing. Why did he think I was expecting something like that? We were talking in the living room before the fire. Ma kept coming in and out. People grew up sooner in my day, Pa said. People aren't even expected to grow up till they're thirty now, and now you're thirty I get the feeling you want to put it off further still. That was Pa's bitterness. He usually doesn't let it come out. It scared me. But I got mad and said people have always been able to pretend they were grown up, but when does anyone grow up? How can he say what grown up is? I told him I was contented with most things already. I like not being ambitious. I like living on a small scale, settled in. I expect to continue to live on this scale the rest of my life. I think he feels I'm waiting to throw everything over like Hannah, run off across the world, pile up hoards of things to keep me busy, a weekend house in the country, dinner parties, trips. Mir wouldn't have wanted those things either. She liked it that I worked in a bookstore, or in the record store, all the jobs I've had. Why did they have to keep thinking it was her doing? It was their doing, I said. I'm tired of hearing it's always the mother's doing, said Ma on one of her trips in. She was exasperated but trying not to be mad or tearful. I didn't say it was the mother's doing, in the sense of blame resting there, I said, or the father's. Blame doesn't rest. Blame traces back and back. I told them that. I'm not trying to blame. They wouldn't feel it was their doing anyway. They know what they did. They had their reasons too. They don't even know what I'm talking about because they wouldn't know love in the way I'm talking about it. It took me a lot of watching to know what I wanted it to be. It was different for them. I think people used to pretend they'd grown up sooner. And here I was living with Mir for five years and making no decision about being able to get married.

I don't understand why you and she gave up. I don't understand how you lived together so long, slept together. I remember visiting you a lot when I first went to college. You'd just moved in together, and you had that big bed. It seemed like a place to sleep with someone. I've always tried to sleep with someone in small beds kneeing each other and falling off the edges, only a night at a time, never enough sleep, have terrible dreams, can't bear sleeping with someone for the terrible dreams I always have.

My dreams were happy when I slept with Mir, peaceful dreams, dreams of this room, dreams of sailing out of it. Let me tell you about the first time I made love, Sim. I want to tell you about it. Is it all right?

Do you want to?

I want to remember it. I want to tell it to you if you won't mind hearing it.

All right, tell me.

Jock and I had brought our girlfriends out after graduation. It was that summer the family was splitting everything up. I was up here in the tower with Essie at sunset, leaning out the windows, looking at things. I pointed out to her where the pagan circle in the woods was. I told her it was a pagan circle made of trees. I was drunk. She thought my family was crazy anyway. I had her all confused about the Norse gods on the walls. She didn't know what I was talking about. We were laughing and carrying on, sitting on this couch. I was making up one of my long involved stories. I was telling her how the whole family was a secret cult. We'd held on to the ancient pagan religion, never been converted, kept our own, passed it down over centuries. What did she think my uncle had painted all these warrior gods and goddesses and gnomes on the walls of our house for! We were all brought up with it. I was brought up with it and didn't know if I believed, I said, but I'd been made to learn, I'd partaken. I told her how when Gramma died, that was only half a year before, well, they had a regular Episcopalian service in town for her society friends, for pretenses, but the family had its own pagan ceremony out here, and we scattered her ashes in the woods in the light of the moon and danced to the rising sun and painted our bodies blue. She was laughing, and we were belting down the beers. Jock and Sarah were making out on the other couch. They weren't listening to us, just wondered why we kept laughing. Of course it was all leading up to something. I knew it perfectly well. I think Essie even mentioned it first: I suppose you deflower virgins in your pagan ceremonies, she said, and I said, oh yes, of course, especially on Midsummer Night, which it practically was. I was terrified and excited and enough drunk to keep joking along these lines. Essie liked the style of the whole thing. You know how it is then. It's the angle you take, the mood. It doesn't spring up from anywhere. You have to establish the mood for it, almost a dare. We ended up leaving Jock and Sarah to their own devices and going down to the costume trunk. We got ourselves all robed up. Ma and Pa and Uncle Tommy and Aunt Judith were playing cards and drinking on the sitting porch, supposedly chaperones. Essie and I dressed up like a couple of barbarians. I don't know what we wore, fur robes, skins, capes. We snuck out a window in one of the bedrooms. I don't know why, could've gone out a door. It was very exciting. We snuck along the side of the house looking at the lights in the windows, ducked down hiding when anyone's shadow appeared in a window, snuck along the wall, got very quiet when we went into the woods, down the lane of pines. The house was like a big gargoyle squatting behind us across the pool. I got sort of scared. Spirits are going to jump out at us, I kept whispering. The moon shone into the woods. I'd never done anything like that before. I was always very reserved. The costumes helped. Essie was one of those dramatic types. You don't remember her, always in plays at school, sophisticated and sure of herself, easily scared in the woods though. We'd been sort of pals senior year, but we'd never really gone out, except after play rehearsals, all in a group. Now what do you do to dance in the moonlight like the pagans, she asked. And we haven't brought any blue paint. We should paint ourselves blue. You know how kids are who remember a few facts from their history courses and consider themselves sophisticated intellectuals. It turned into sort of a wrestling match. It started off as a dance. The costumes started coming off. I had some odd silky balloony trousers on, which were hell to get out of in the process of wrestling around without being obvious that was what I was doing. I don't know why with all that cloth we didn't end up lying on it, but we kept getting nakeder and nakeder on the itchy grass. We kept rolling around. Let's paint ourselves blue anyway, she said. So we pretended we were painting ourselves with our tongues, and I ended up painting her blue, and she painted me blue, and by that point our underwear had come off too, but we didn't quite do anything yet because she said now we have to dance naked in the moonlight. She liked to dance free-form. I just

stood there sort of and helped her balance. I was very excited by the whole thing, but I still felt unsure. She was
drunk enough so she fell down soon, and then I do feel I was
somehow possessed by a pagan spirit, drunkenly that's
what I told myself, because I began to act in a way I'd never
acted. I said: Now the time for the sacrifice has come, to
Thee Wotan, something ridiculous like that. I wasn't even
being funny. I was very serious and drunk. I became very
strong. I've never felt strong. I became very strong and hard.
I couldn't imagine doing it the way Jock and Sarah were
doing it, on that couch, all cramped in there, the thing
rocking and scraping, anybody coming in at any minute. I'd
have ended up giggling over it, but out in the woods we had
got all our giggles out of us and it was suddenly serious, and
I became for the moment the person I am in my dreams
where I can sail out over everything, some sense of power.
Essie felt it too. I knew she couldn't be hurt by this sort of
thing. She would not be hurt. I'd always felt before that the
girl would be hurt. Suddenly I didn't feel that was so. She
was powerful too. And then in lovemaking, all that silliness
of Wotan and blue pagans went away, and I didn't think of
them anymore. I thought of this strange single creature in
the woods that comes together and comes apart and shoves
into itself and takes its own self into itself and makes
moans from two mouths, and this went on for some time,
and hardly even finished before it had to start again, and it
got later, and whatever had happened with Jock and Sarah
must've been over too, and the single blue creature in the
woods got stiller and stiller and began to remember it had
been dressed up as a barbarian, and that its odd clothes were
scattered on the grass, and that the moon had passed behind
the trees, it was itchy and even somewhat cold, and it had
done what it had had to do.

PART TWO

◆

Conversation
(Sim, Aunt Abby, later Dan)

Do you want help with anything, Aunt Abby?

Hello, Simmy. Did you get a shower? I don't think I want any help. You might put the bread on the breadboard and put it on the table. Take that knife there. Is Danny showering?

He'll be done in a minute.

Did you have enough hot? We've such a small tank.

Dan likes cold showers.

Toby has a cold shower every morning, in the depth of winter even. I wait till he's got the kitchen fire going before I dare hop out of bed. I'm the old softy. You don't mind eating in the kitchen? It's lazy of me when my two grandnephews visit for the first time in ten years, having dinner at the kitchen table, but you don't mind?

I like eating in the kitchen.

Toby and I are the family oddities. It's not a bad reputation to have. We do our best to foster it. Not as much is expected of us. Maybe you can help me get the casserole out of the oven, Simmy.

I'll do it, Aunt Abby. Where's the other pot holder?

This is Toby's casserole, his very own secret concoction. He gets it all started when I'm having my nap. All I have to do is take it out at the proper time. Toby keeps busy every minute, and I fiddle about the house, get the worst of the dust up. That's the extent of it.

I like your house. It's cozy with stuff everywhere.

I don't know where to put things. They pile up.

You know what was on the bedside table in our room? Ten copies of Gramma's obituary. They were between a couple of books in a pile.

I'm sure they've been there since she died. I don't often straighten up in there. If it's in a pile, I leave it. Toby's always stashing things. He has his projects everywhere.

It's nice this way. I like it.

And how do you live, Simmy?

How do I live?

What's it like where you live? I don't know you at all. Last time I saw you, I remember it, all five of you were back here for a visit. You were thirteen, came in from playing tennis in your white shorts, and I thought Simmy's still got a little boy's hairless little legs. Am I embarrassing you?

No.

But Danny hasn't changed much to my eyes. He was as big then as he is now. His forehead's higher, his skin's rougher, he's skinnier than he was, that's all, but now you're even a bit taller than he is, your voice is deeper than his, and you were a stubby little fellow, so quiet, seemed younger than you were.

You probably didn't know me much when I was little. I stuck to myself mostly.

I remember your Aunt Judith taking me aside, with ostensible concern, but she loved to gossip. Don't you think

Simmy's an odd child, she'd say, playing off by himself so much? Don't you think we should make a special effort to bring him into things, Aunt Abby?

I dreaded Aunt Judith then.

Your ma had terrible times with her, but I've never taken Judith seriously. There, the shower's off. Now I can wash the lettuce, didn't want to unbalance Danny's shower. Tell me about your apartment, Simmy. I want to be able to imagine how you live.

I was lucky to find it. Rents keep going up. It's just a little place, one room with a sort of alcove for the bed.

I can't imagine what sort of home you'd make for yourself. Are you a stasher like Toby? Are there piles of things everywhere?

I'm sort of tidy. I don't keep much stuff. I like it the way you have it, but I'm never able to have things that way. I always throw stuff out. Dan's more of a stasher, but organized. Everything's got its drawer, the books and records are alphabetized.

Let me have those tomatoes, Simmy. But I want to hear about you, not Danny. Now, do you have a girlfriend? That's what I'd like to know.

No.

Am I embarrassing you, a prying old great-aunt?

No, no, I just don't have one.

Hester's letters haven't given a clue. She writes about your doing so well at school, getting the job next year.

It may not be what I really want to do.

Hester tells me about all that, but she hasn't said a thing about a girl, or about friends at all. I don't have a sense of what you like to do.

I have a number of friends at the Ed School. We play

tennis, play soccer. Most of my college friends have gone elsewhere. It's been a low year that way. I see people from the Ed School, but I don't have any particularly close friends right now. There are people I go to movies with. The work keeps me busy.

I don't get a sense of it, Simmy. I'm curious. I can't help it. You don't mind supermarket salad dressing? Set that on the table. Is there a mistake you keep making, Simmy? Do things keep happening a certain way?

Maybe I tend to pick the sort of people who move off. I'm struck with them at first. I'm afraid of them a bit, so I force myself to pick out that sort.

I wish you'd give me examples to give me more of a feeling. Who was your roommate at college? What was his name?

One of my roommates was Squinty, it's what we called him.

Were you good friends?

He had a lot of friends who lived off campus. He lives on a communal farm now. Not too many people still do that sort of thing. We didn't keep in touch. He regarded me as his straight roommate. At first he thought he was going to make a convert of me. That's when we got to be friends. Then we were stuck rooming together, but he was off campus most of the time. Last time I saw him he was mad at me because I wouldn't lend him money. I was better friends with our other roommate. He was the hardworking sort. He's off at law school now. I heard from him once or twice.

Which of the girls you knew did you like best?

There was one I went out with a couple of times. She was involved with a guy who was taking a semester in England.

She lived down the hall. I spent a good deal of time with her for a while. None of it sounds like the way things were when you were in college, does it, Aunt Abby?

I know how things work these days.

I should force myself more.

Why do you worry so about forcing yourself, Simmy? This is not the sort of thing that should be forced. It should appeal to you.

If I don't force myself, I don't do anything. That's the worst thing about me. I always have to keep forcing myself.

But it doesn't relax you. I don't think you should make a project of it. Maybe I don't understand. Well, here's Danny, fresh from a cold shower.

What don't you understand, Aunt Ab?

I'm just gurgling away about my declining state.

I like cold showers. Feel awake again. I was very sleepy this afternoon. I don't usually get sleepy in the middle of the day.

I'd think you both might be sleepy, trudging through that old house, every nook and cranny.

It looks like dinner's ready. Where's Uncle Tobe? I'd like to dive into that casserole.

Why don't you go find him, Danny? He's somewhere in the barn. It'll take you ten minutes at least to get him moving. You'd better go right now. Simmy, will you get the wine out of the icebox and pour it around? I'll just tidy up a bit.

For some reason, Sim, I'm very awake and nervous. I'm relieved we've seen the house and it's over. I feel like something else has to begin. Oh, a big jug, just what's called for. I think I'll get sloshed, that's how I feel. It's funny, I haven't felt this way in a while. Pour me one quick sip first. That's good. I'll go hurry up the old codger in the barn.

(Uncle Toby, Dan)

Who's that stumbling around out there?

It's Dan. It's dinnertime, Uncle Tobe. What's that you're working on?

You ought to recognize this, Daniel.

It's the other chandelier.

It's the other chandelier, that's what it is. Armless as yet, pitted with rot, but in the process of restoration. I have a commission. The Brothers can't do with an unbalanced Great Hall, so they've come to the Master Builder himself, and though considerably enfeebled he has promised to restore the torso and hang it up there opposite its mate. I've had to turn out new little nubbins on my lathe, epoxy them on, look at this, and you'll never know the finished piece isn't carved from one solid trunk. And then I have to match the finish, attach the arms. It's quite a project for an old man.

Where are the arms?

I fear your grandfather never got around to pounding out the second set. He died, stepped right out of the forge one summer afternoon, came inside feeling tired, never got up again. I attached the arms he'd finished, and the other armless body got stashed for twenty-five years in a leaky garage. One of the Brothers came across it under some old tires, puzzled over it, recognized it for what it was, and in time brought it to me. Odd to think of restoration going on in the old castle at this early date. Even some Rhine castles don't get this kind of attention. I'm forced to have the new arms manufactured. I'd like to heat up the old forge myself, but I concede I'm a bit past it. However, I'm tempted to offer to touch up my tower mural into the bargain. I understand it's fading. What's that?

Napkin ring, I was twiddling with it, must've brought it along.

A napkin ring of my own making, I might point out, turned out on my lathe. Don't lose track of it, get it back to its napkin. Things get lost around here. Does dinner smell good? I have to do everything for your poor great-aunt. It's all she can do to get through a day. We're both seventy-eight, you know. Here, hold this.

Here?

Now don't let it slip. See what a delicate operation this is? Don't budge. Do you think it's worth my interrupting these labors to come to dinner?

For the company alone.

Now let that go. There, isn't that fine! Only two more.

Aunt Ab'll get impatient about dinner.

When have I ever come to dinner on time? When dinner is announced, she still takes ten minutes to tidy herself. Perhaps you're the impatient one.

I'm a little starved.

We'll effect a compromise, one more nubbin instead of two. Stand back while I cut this. A steady hand for an old man. Hold this.

I wanted to ask you about your mural, Uncle Tobe.

It could do with a touch-up, couldn't it? I'll try to weasel another commission, perhaps.

What was Ma in your mural?

Can you still make her out? She was fading when last I saw her.

She was almost gone, but her hands were there holding

a string and those big shears. I remember how it used
to look.

Hester was one of the Norns. You're familiar with the
Norns? Imagine my painting such a piece of Germanism
during the war! Barbarous! What got into me? But I saw no
reason I should allow Mr. Hitler to appropriate my own
gods. They were mine long before I'd ever heard of Mr.
Hitler. Your ma had just married into the family when I
needed my youngest Norn. My old sister Mary, you remember her, she was the Norn of the Past, my dear wife was the
Norn of the Present. I'm afraid I've forgotten their mythical
names after all these years. And we landed Hester in time
for her to fill out the trio. An aging spinster, a childless wife
approaching middle age, and a blushing bride! The war was
beginning, not a thing certain. We didn't know who'd come
out of it alive. Can you imagine the state of things before
you were born? There I was, putting the whole family up on
the wall, attired as my gods. They were all there, watching
the giants' legs, which supported a colossal fight in midair
somewhere above the tower out of sight. Now hold this.
Don't budge.

Who are they all supposed to be? I've forgotten.

It's a famous mythological scene, surely you remember,
Daniel. Freia, that's your Aunt Maddy, is bound up for ran-
som, the goddess of love and beauty, poor Maddy, and her
brother Froh, peace and happiness, that's Joseph your pa,
he's setting her free. Then Tommy's storming about the
place as Donner, the war god, and Jake, well, Mr. Hitler put
an end to him soon enough, I put him in as Loge, the magic-
fire god, the trickster, for all his gadgetry and secret passageways. My brother and his wife sit enthroned watching
the combat between the giants, who had built them their

dream castle on the cliffs above the Rhine. Don't let that
slip, Daniel. Let me clamp it. Clever of me to show only
those pairs of hairy legs, to make you imagine the giant
torsos beyond the roof. And where do you think I am? That's
me sneaking up the wall of the stairwell, Alberich, the
gnome-king, the one who renounced love for the sake of
power.

That's hardly like you, Uncle Tobe.

Hardly like me at all, indeed, well, enough of this. The
rest of the family certainly never gave any thought to the
allegory I put them in. Now let that piece go.

You put Edna in the mural too.

Of course I put Edna in. Edna had brought the four of
them up. How she had filled little Jake full of doom! What
tales of the Kaiser and the Hun! And we all went to Berlin in
'thirty-six, all of us, Mary and Abby and I, too, the Poore
clan in fact, with Edna shaking in her shoes looking after
Jake. Daniel footed the bill, the Bayreuth Festival, the
Olympics. Yes, and we saw Mr. Hitler himself, a little speck
at a great distance. That's how I think of him to this day.
Jake was only ten. He was scared to leave the hotel room. He
was obsessed with Nazis ever after. He studied their uni-
forms, their insignia, their weaponry. Of course, he was
right to have been obsessed. I wonder what he used to
imagine went on in his castle keep and secret passageways,
what was being done to whom down there. Jake was a scary
boy, you might not have known that. I found him unset-
tling. And of course I put the old brown-skinned lady in a
corner of my mural, rising out of the earth, foretelling the
dusk of the gods. You must know how it goes in the opera.
We sat through the entire Ring that trip. Abby fell asleep, for
which I forgave her, she has no ear, but my old sister Mary,

you remember her still, she took a delightful view of it all. You know the part where Brünnhilde is made to sleep surrounded by magic fire with her great round shield resting upon her bosom. Mary turned to me and whispered, much too loudly: Brünnhilde en casserole! Speaking of which, it's time for dinner. I think that will hold now.

(All Four)

Did you make these napkin rings, Uncle Toby?

Of course I did, Simeon, turned them out on my lathe. I'll turn you out something someday.

You have enough projects, Toby.

No one has enough projects, Abbess, quite impossible to have.

Uncle Toby's restoring the other chandelier, Sim, on a commission.

Do let's have some more Rhenish to wash down the last of the dinner. Pass it around, Simeon.

I'm a little fuzzy. I'll stop there. Here, Dan.

Sim's easily drunk, Uncle Tobe.

But one should indulge. How better to end a good hard day?

What was your song, you used to lie under the piano after dinner and sing it, Uncle Tobe?

Don't get him started, Danny.

AWAY, AWAY WITH RUM, BY GUM!

That's it.

AWAY, AWAY WITH RUM!

Toby, stop it.

Maybe I'll have just a sip, Dan. I'm very sleepy though.

I remember what else you used to do, Uncle Tobe, pretending you could play the piano.

One of my clever deceptions, couldn't play a note otherwise, taught myself purely mechanically, the opening bars of some rather difficult and well-known sonatas. I'd play a couple of impressive measures, everyone would look around, I'd slam down the lid over the keys, temperamentally: I don't feel like playing right now, I'd say, get up and storm out of the room.

Some of my lady friends still won't believe Toby isn't a virtuoso.

I remember you singing away on the floor under the piano at Gramma's.

AWAY, AWAY WITH RUM!

And when we came back to the house after Gramma's funeral.

I suppose I did, Daniel. It's odd how one behaves after funerals, not as one would expect. I've always been outlandish.

That's how you'd love to see yourself, Toby, you know it. He writes the most devilish letters to his namesake, Maddy's Toby. He loves to play the bad old great-uncle.

I haven't seen that boy since he was a mite. Maddy sends pictures. I don't want him to turn dull, that's all, Abbess, living out in the woods with slow-moving Maddy, never hearing from his father. I write him all manner of things to keep him snappy. I write him about his father. I'm sure no one else dares so much as mention his father to him.

What was Uncle David like, Uncle Toby?

It's funny to hear you call him Uncle David, Simmy.

I don't know what to call him. I vaguely remember him. He was very thin and never really spoke to me.

An evasive character, Simeon, kept going off on archae-
ological digs. Maddy never got along with him. I trust he's
off riding a camel somewhere now. Now Joseph was marvelous with Maddy, fellows, always had been. He always
knew where she was, what she was doing. It wasn't tyranni-
cal on his part, it was a comfort. He found David for Maddy,
unfortunate mistake that it was. Joseph still feels bad about
it, or Maddy worries that he does. She's still very attached to
your pa. She writes us often, doesn't she, Abbess? We hear
more from her than from anyone. Joseph had tried so hard to
find someone for his sister, and now she's up in her woods. A
little more Rhenish, Simeon?

Well, half a glass.

I feel I must call you Simeon, and you Daniel. I can't bear
the Simmy and Danny my wife resorts to.

I can't break the habit, Toby. They were Simmy and
Danny when we last saw them.

Diminutives are the great-aunt's prerogative, Abbess, I'll
grant you. The great-uncle must set a sterner tone. Look at
my letters to little Toby. Toby, you notice, still Toby, still
a boy. I always sign them Your Overbearing Great-uncle
Tobias. I encourage him to write me everything he's thinking. Sometimes I goad him into a fury. He writes very boldly
back. Well, that's between him and me, I mustn't make
public business of it.

I worry that Toby pushes things a bit far at times. He
prides himself on his instincts so, but I'd be carefuller.

Of course you would, Abbess. You're a careful soul. I've
never been. These things need risking. Better he should
grow to hate that old blowhard of a Great-uncle Tobias than
not know him. I've stashed all his letters away. They're
precious to me.

But you won't think of traveling up to see him, you're such a stay-at-home.

Oh, Abbess, but then he'd see me as a wretched old man, stumbling about, singing drunkenly on his back under the piano. I choose to remain imaginary.

But think how marvelous it is to see these two here again. All we get otherwise is polite duty calls from Jake and Tom. Hannah's never back here. She successfully escaped.

My, Abbess, how you do carry on! Polite duty calls!

Toby, you know how Judith nudges those sons of hers.

Abbess, I grant you, we're neither of us particularly fond of Judith, but maligning her has become an obsession with you.

I thought you were the one who barred nothing, Uncle Tobe.

Oh, Danny, he's just ribbing me. It is one of my obsessions, he's right. I never tire of it.

A little ribbing keeps one snappy. More?

If I have any more, I'm easily affected by wine, I don't know why.

Go on, Sim, you're funny when you get a little sloshy.

Here, Simeon, I'll just top you off once more. Daniel?

Why not.

Abbess?

I've hardly touched what I have, Toby.

And by the way, Abbess, since you mention her, shouldn't we ask the fellows more about their escaped sister?

We never hear anything from Hannah, you know. She writes Ma and Pa from time to time. We read those, I do anyway. I'm not sure if she's a terrible letter writer or if she would just as soon forget her brothers.

She wouldn't just as soon forget us, Dan. She's busy with

her own doings. Some people don't write letters. I wouldn't
be good at it.

I don't care how busy she is. She should write us, Sim. I
write her. I refuse to keep reading the news filtered through
Ma and Pa.

But this is a phenomenon, Daniel. She doesn't write you!

Toby and I've never met Matt. We don't have an idea of
what he's like. Your Aunt Judith was very impressed with
him, I know. I think she senses your ma is upset about
Hannah being off in England and gloats over it.

I tell you, you can't keep Abbess off the subject of Judith.

But what is Matt like, Danny? He's a handsome man in
pictures.

You'd like Matt. He's full of enthusiasm.

I don't like Matt that much.

A differing point of view from Simeon!

He gets too heated up. They're always picking at each
other. Then they both yell and storm around. Their way of
doing things is very explosive.

The well-known Anglo-Saxon reserve, I've heard tell of it,
Simeon.

It isn't just Matt though, Sim. Hannah's explosive too.
She was always temperamental. She always had that famous glower.

Yes, indeed, we remember her glower, don't we, Toby? As
a little girl she could cast such glances, positively withering.

And she isn't good at smoothing things over. You know
how she feels by her face. She'd think she was disguising it,
but there it was. Matt brings it all out. Sim's right, they can
go at each other. I'm not used to that sort of thing. We don't
see enough of them though. They only come over on quick

trips. Hannah always gets upset at first when she sees us. She imagines what it would've been like if she'd stayed here. She gets wistful, cries, gets Ma all wrought up. Then she calms down. When the time comes she's always glad to get back on the plane.

She doesn't write Dan or me because it makes her homesick to write, that's what I think. She imagines we're doing things she wishes she could be doing, having completely happy normal American lives. If she knew what we really had, she'd be glad to be where she is with Matt and their parties and country house and trips.

Things look better from the other side of an ocean, the history of the human race, Simeon.

Sim tries to understand Hannah more than I do. I'm mad at her. I've decided not to try to do anything anymore. I've tried to keep in touch. I've tried to help her talk about her problems, give advice. She doesn't follow it.

But Simmy has a point, Danny. You can understand how homesick Hannah must be to have uprooted herself. None of her own family, her familiar ways.

Abbess, don't be flimsy about this. She only increases the homesickness by not writing, difficult though it may be. There's something wrong. The young woman should not have excuses made for her. This damn family is flimsy to the bone, always thought so. Lazy, flimsy, won't pursue things, the most unruffled tribe I know, won't dig underneath, finds an excuse and stops there. And your parents are the worst of the lot, fellows, I don't care if I raise your hackles by saying so. They're my dear favorite nephew and his sweet dear wife, both of whom I've always loved. I'm a sentimental old man, but I rise above it and speak with authority. They never knew what they thought, never knew what they wanted, never did. They never even knew if they wanted to be parents. How's that strike you? They became parents, of course. What else could they consider? It would've been harder to decide not to back then, take it from two of us who did decide. We could've been parents, indeed, at one point we were going to be and decided to prevent it. Do I horrify you both? We took some time to understand our natures. It's not something I intend to go into. It's a painful and private matter between my old wife and me. Look at her staring into her lap, furious at me for telling you these things. But I want to let you know that such decisions can be made. And when I think of Joseph and Hester, and here before me sit their eldest and youngest, I must confess I don't sense that you were intensely desired.

What a thing to say, Toby!

You know how I love to say unspeakable things, Abbess. I want the fellows to think about them. They've learned too much unruffledness. They explain things. I've noticed it in both of them. It's put them quite adrift. I see them suffering under it. Daniel sounded so like Joseph at lunch, making self-effacing jokes about the recent disasters in his life, losing a job, deserted by the woman he's lived with for five years, the woman he's put through school.

Toby, don't keep pressing this. Too much wine.

Nonsense, Abbess. We've spoken of it between ourselves often enough, no reason not to speak of it to the two fellows. And Simeon requires it as much as Daniel does. I do mean to shake him a bit. He's anxious to explain things for his sister's sake, but what does he want for himself? An unloving sister?

Toby, this is absolutely enough. The coffee's ready.

I'll help clear, Aunt Ab.

No, sit, Danny.

No, I'll help.

I intend to sit, Abbess.

I trust you've been silenced for a while, Toby. Set the plates on the counter, Danny. Toby's cookies are in the jar in the pantry if you'd like to get them.

Hermits, Daniel, hermits like the man that made them.

Set the plates here, thank you, Danny.

Should I just bring out the cookie jar?

By all means, bring the jar, Daniel.

Sugar and cream, Danny?

Yes, thanks.

Abbess, you mustn't look at me so reproachfully.

But we only have this one evening to talk with them.

Precisely.

But don't attack Simmy. You don't know him well enough. You don't know how you affect him. I'm going to change the subject.

Abbess, I will not have the subject changed.

Too much wine.

AWAY, AWAY WITH RUM, BY GUM!

Have some coffee, Simmy. Do you want anything in it?

Black.

And have one of my hermits.

You can go on with what you were saying, Uncle Toby. I wasn't upset by it, Aunt Abby. It's what I was saying about being a mistake, Dan. Uncle Toby was sort of saying the same thing, but for all of us.

But what do we know of Joseph and Hester, Toby? What did we know of them then? What do we know of them as they are? Hester's letters reveal so little.

They're happier than they were back here, Aunt Ab. Sim

and I both think so. They won't come up to see us in the city
for anything. They like us to come down to the beach. You
know how they are. They don't like it much outside their
own setting.

As I was saying, Abbess.

Toby, be quiet for a while. Let me hear it from the boys.
And Joseph and Hester aren't lonely being there year-round?

They like to be by themselves.

They sound much like us, Toby.

But they don't talk about things the way you do. They
don't talk about things much at all.

What do they talk about, Daniel?

They don't talk about anything. You can't talk to them.
You can only talk to them about their latest projects.

And what did your friend Miriam think of them?

She didn't know how they felt about her. She didn't like to
go there. We didn't go often. If I went down it was more
likely with Sim, or alone.

But how was it when Miriam did come, Danny, that's
what I want to know.

I don't know. It was awkward. Ma never lets anyone help
her in the kitchen. Mir wanted to help, felt sort of useless.
Ma doesn't let anyone do anything. I never try. The most I
do is empty the dishwasher after she's gone to bed, but I
think she'd as soon I didn't even do that. There's nothing to
do in the house because they do it all. You can't help. They
don't need anything. Pa's as bad about the outdoors, can't
help him around the place. Sim just goes sailing and I take
walks, or sit around and read, and eat and drink. It's pleasant
enough. They wouldn't sit around and talk over dinner like
this. They putter about, both of them, adding a little here or
there, changing this or that. They don't let things pile up the

way you do. Everything goes into their setting, working over it inch by inch, everything has its most perfect possible place, a little shelf exactly the right size for the salt dishes.

Perhaps they've reached the stage they should have chosen from the start, fellows: childlessness, again at last sufficient unto themselves.

It was the war that made it hard for Joseph and Hester, Toby, I've often thought. It made a frightening rush out of things. They might have waited a bit if they hadn't felt they had to get Danny started. It's something you boys can't imagine, how much the war made people do things.

Pa never talks about the war.

Your grandfather and I, neither of us made it over in the first war. We might have eventually, but it ended. We have no tales to tell. I'm sure your pa has them, but no, he wouldn't tell.

What were Ma and Pa like when they were young? I don't have much of a picture of them. I was thinking this afternoon how Pa ran around that place when he was a kid too. I can't imagine it.

Joseph used to occupy himself in the garden, clipping bushes, digging little trenches around the flower beds. Remember him doing that, Abbess? Mindless little things, spent hours at it, worrying about getting this branch exactly even with that one, down to the inch.

And, of course, we didn't know Hester till she came into the family. I took to her immediately. She was a shy girl, with nothing in the way of family of her own. She was quite overwhelmed by the lot of us, wanted very much to be liked. So opposite from Judith, Toby, you'll have to admit. Judith never tried to get the spirit of things.

I will grant I was a bit annoyed she wouldn't allow me to

add her face to my mural. It was after the war when Tommy finally married. I could've stuck her in as some sort of Valkyrie galloping across the sky, but she wouldn't hear of it.

But how charming Hester was when Joseph brought her here to visit us the first time. Of course Joseph was our favorite nephew, and so we were predisposed. It's remarkable how you can recognize when someone has found the right person. I'm as sensitive as a bat to it.

Indeed, and even on first meeting, eh, Abbess? I wonder how well you remember being introduced to me at school, the man you would spend the next sixty years of your life with. An appalling bit of chance!

(Dan, Uncle Toby, Sim)

Shouldn't we get Aunt Ab to come watch?

She's happy with the dishes. It's her little respite after dinner, tidying up. What's this say, Simeon?

Tobogganing.

That's not what I'm looking for.

Let's see it, Uncle Tobe.

But I'm looking for the eightieth birthday. What's this say?

Tommy's wedding.

Abbess wouldn't stand for me showing that one. Judith in her glory.

Show the tobogganing one, Uncle Tobe. I remember seeing it years ago. It has Ma and Pa when they were young.

But where's the eightieth birthday? Your great-grand-mother, our medieval costumes. I myself make an appearance at a considerably earlier age. I must make a project of organizing the back of this closet.

Here it is, Uncle Toby. Hannah Poore, Eightieth Birthday, Nineteen Forty.

I was afraid it had been tucked off in some corner.

Show the tobogganing one first, Uncle Tobe.

If you're so insistent, Daniel, but it goes by awfully fast, not much more than a glimpse. Tommy and Judith were still courting, Joseph and Hester chaperoning them, if I may call it that. Can a younger brother be said to be a chaperone? You may turn off the lights, Daniel. Here it comes. Is it focused? My eyes aren't entirely accurate.

It's in color.

Surprising, isn't it, Simeon, in something so antique.

The color's bluish. That's the meadow, recognize it, Sim? The snow looks blue. I wish we'd walked out there today. It was too deep.

Is it focused?

It's fine, Uncle Tobe. Look, Sim, there's the tower peeking out of the trees.

Where? Oh yes.

The gully's over to the left, out of the picture, Tannu Tuva, covered with snow.

What's off to the left, Daniel?

There's Ma, Dan!

Look at her in that fuzzy hat. I remember that hat. How old was Ma then? She was younger than I am now, younger than Mir.

Pa's getting on behind, shoving off, whoa, there they go. Whoa, over they went!

Here they come trudging back up. Where are Uncle Tommy and Aunt Judith?

Judith was not much of a sportswoman. Here she is. Now watch Tommy coax her. Perhaps you fellows can observe how smitten he was.

What's he doing with a fedora or whatever you call those hats when he's going tobogganing?

Simeon, tolerate the styles of the past. You'll look peculiar someday too.

There she goes! She doesn't like it.

Uncle Tommy's falling off. He was fat then. Do you remember him so fat, Dan?

I still think of him as fat.

As life disappointed him, fellows, he thinned.

Aunt Judith isn't enjoying this at all, Sim. Oh, she pushed him in the snow.

Look at Aunt Judith and Uncle Tommy! She's down, she's got him by the ankle, he's dragging her along. Aunt Judith!

Isn't there a shot of you, Uncle Tobe?

I remain unseen. Here you watch the events of some twenty-eight years ago. There's no evidence of my presence, but I was there. In fact, you're seeing with my eyes.

Look, Ma's going down backwards! I can't believe that's Ma.

That's Ma, Sim.

She wouldn't do something like that!

Hester was daring, Simeon, when she wanted to be. She couldn't pass a chance to show up Judith. And Hannah just born!

Is it over?

That's it, a mere glimpse.

It just came to a stop.

Ran out of film. Lights, Daniel. Which of these damn buttons do I push?

Whoa, it's flipping around.

Where's that eightieth birthday? Now this takes us further back. World War Two separates these little movies. Hester won't be in this one. You won't know half the people here. Most of them are dead, some are too far removed. You'll catch a glimpse or two of Abbess. Your great-aunt didn't enjoy being photographed. Watch her dart out of camera range. Have I inserted this properly? Lights, Daniel. This one's in black and white.

The trees are smaller around the house.

They are, Simeon, you who spent so much time sitting under them. Ah, my new building, my gargoyles, my archways, and there, Maddy's studio, the crab apple trees, blossoms falling in the wading pool. Your great-grandmother was born in the spring, fellows.

Who's that?

These are preparations. That's some second cousin. Mama was up the road at this house. Abbess had invited her for a quiet lunch. She didn't expect anyone to make much of her birthday. Now watch, there's Tommy. He's off to pick her up in the Packard. That car had mushrooms growing in the moldy backseat. Its roof leaked.

That's the Packard before the Packard I remember. That's Aunt Mary.

You do remember her, Daniel. Indeed, that's sister Mary. Simeon, are you taking all this in?

Mmm.

Mary's putting on witch's robes. She didn't want to be merely another lady-in-waiting. We all had to be medieval, one way or another.

These are some of the costumes from the costume trunk, Sim. I remember those costumes.

Oh, Abbess, Mary, Bess too, they spent secret hours sewing away. There's Bess.

There's Gramma.

One of those pointed hats with the lace attached at the top, whatever you call them.

We were thorough in our games, Daniel. We prepared months for such an event. Now the scene shifts, through the archway, the Packard, that's young Jake and a young second cousin, riding the running boards. Look at their armor, swords in hand! The car halts and the throng closes in. Look at Mama, peering out. She was a tiny little lady. That's your great-grandmother, fellows.

I do remember this movie. I remember seeing her before.

Daniel, lord of the castle, steps up to welcome her, helps her down.

That's Aunt Maddy.

That's Maddy, a chubby eighteen. The others are second cousins.

Who's that little girl?

That's Mama's sister's son's daughter. You'd hardly know what she is to you, too far removed. She has the crown. Mama bends down.

This is wonderful, Uncle Tobe. We should've had something like this for Gramma.

Now they parade her through the courtyard and out onto the terrace.

Are we going to see you, Uncle Tobe?

I passed the camera over to little Jake at one point. He was mad for filming. There's Abbess, see, she darts right out of my range. And there I am. Don't I look fierce in my helmet and furs! I was a mad warlord from the outlands, not yet

entirely subdued. Look at the villainous twisty mustache!
Jake wobbles the camera around too much. The camera
must be back in my hands, the wobbling's stopped. Mama
looks confused. She's so tiny, and with that crown on her
head!

She's smiling.

But timidly, Simeon.

There goes Aunt Ab again, out of the picture.

So uncooperative. Don't point that thing at me, Toby, I
can hear her saying, don't point that thing at me! Ah, now
we get a fine sequence of your grandfather. There he is. His
lordliest manner. He loved to take this part. He takes Mama
by the hand.

I've never seen our grandfather moving before, just old
pictures Pa has. He doesn't look as stern in this. Dan remembers him, but I wasn't born yet.

Look, there he is with the sun in his eyes. He's very tall.

And we lead the old dowager into the house. There's Jake
with his sword.

There's Edna.

She had to have a costume too, grumped about the whole
thing. There goes the procession into the house. Maddy and
Tommy, and there's Joseph at last.

There's Pa in one of the robes from the costume trunk.

He looks glum. He always looked rather glum as a young
man, sloping off. My wife once again ducking out of range.
What's this now?

It's summer suddenly, the big pool. Look how short the
pines are.

Must be some footage I spliced on at the end. Oh yes, the
croquet game. Hester's in this one. Joseph had begun bringing her out here on weekends.

Uncle Tommy was even fatter then.

There's Ma, Dan.

She does look lovely, fellows. Do you recognize your young ma? Maddy and Hester got along well. Maddy was dying for a sister. Look at them together.

There's Uncle Tommy with his dimples whacking the ball.

He hits Ma's.

Look at Hester's face. Tommy loved to torment her. Look at his vengeful smirk. Here he goes, whack! Off into the woods.

There's Pa down at the other end of the croquet lawn. Who's that?

Uncle Jake, Sim. Look at him dancing around with his mallet, leaping up and down. What's he doing? Aunt Maddy's laughing at him. Look at Ma. Uncle Jake's leaping up and down, swinging his mallet around his head. What a wild man!

There we have it. Lights, Daniel.

(Uncle Toby, Sim)

Yggdrasill. Odd word!

What?

I wonder how it's properly pronounced. Ygg-dra-sill. I'd forgotten it. Quite perturbing when Daniel asked me about my mural. I thought I should refresh my memory. Go on with your puzzle, Simeon. Put it together before Dan comes back from his walk. I'm just looking up a few things. This is a tome to lug about. Better sit down with it.

What book is it, Uncle Toby?

My old mythology. I used to study it with a passion. It belonged to my father. How's the puzzle?

You're a devil with a jigsaw, Uncle Toby.

I used to remember things. How could I forget Yggdrasill? The world-ash tree, its branches spreading out over the heavens and its roots reaching into the earth to all the realms and races of the world, it says here.

Is that the tree I'm sitting under in the mural? Dan pointed out where I was.

I put you in as a little gnome peeking over the roots of the world-ash tree. I never got to add Maddy's Toby. We sold the house before he was old enough.

There they go, these three pieces. There's one. Did Aunt Abby go upstairs already?

She's putting on her snuggies. She'll be down to say good night.

Dan should be in soon. It's a little cold for walking.

Ah, here they are: Urth, Verthandi, Skuld, those were their three names. How could I have forgotten?

♦

Are you falling asleep, Simeon?

No, just looking out. It's clear. The moon's on the snow.

I have a sense we're due for one more big winter storm, Simeon.

I feel wide awake from all the coffee. I don't feel sleepy at all. I feel restless in a way.

Run outside and find your brother.

Too cold.

And where is your old great-aunt? She should be down by now. I'll add a log to the fire.

♦

The wind's picking up.

The wind's picking up, Simeon?

The tops of the trees are whipping about. It was still this afternoon.

I hope you fellows won't have any trouble getting up to Madison to see Daniel's friend. The new interstate takes you right up the valley. Your great-aunt is unnerved when we drive on it. The merging bothers her. We're bound to kill ourselves one day. Why don't you both come back here after visiting what's Daniel's friend's name?

Jock.

Oh yes, Jock, the scientific one. Well, come back down here after visiting Jock, before you head back east.

There's not going to be time, I've got to get back to school. The whole trip's been a last-minute rush. I've got a paper due. You can really hear this wind.

The fire's crackling. I'll stick close to the fire. ABBESS, THE FIRE'S BLAZING AWAY. PUT YOUR SNUGGIES ON AND COME DOWN! She must be on the pot.

◆

Hugin and Munin. I wonder how you pronounce them properly.

Are you still looking things up, Uncle Toby?

Hugin and Munin are Wotan's ravens. They're in my mural too. Hugin and Munin, Thought and Memory. I'd forgotten. I wonder if Fricka's sheep have names. What grade will you be teaching next year, Simeon?

Sixth.

Teach them some mythology. They love it at that age. Does anyone teach mythology these days?

There's a unit on mythology in one of the programs.

And may I ask what a unit is?

It's how they divide the programs, a curriculum-planning thing, you know, but you don't have to follow it exactly.

But Simeon, I'm appalled! What language are you speaking? Don't you have plain books you read?

They try to plan it out in a way.

I don't know this new world.

No, you're right, Uncle Toby, I'd like to give them some mythology. There must be some good book for kids. I'll look around. I've been looking for different sorts of ideas. I haven't read that much myself is the problem. Maybe you could write me some names of books you know.

It will be all I can do to restrain myself from overwhelming you with names of books.

We have to order student editions is the problem. Listen to the wind now.

Come over by the fire, Simeon. Warm up. That window's awfully leaky. Look through this old tome. It's got all the stories of all the different creations of the world.

◆

I hear the pot flushing. Abbess will be down in a moment.

This is a little too much for sixth graders. I'd have to find a more abridged version.

No doubt.

It's interesting. I like the engravings. They remind me of your mural.

I'm a shameless plagiarist. A bit from here, a bit from there. My school of architecture might best have been called Midwestern Bastard.

I never knew what other buildings you built.

I never built whole buildings. Daniel's was the only one I

did from scratch, and even then I had a barn and silo and corncrib to work from. I made my reputation as a remodeler, a restorer. I'd add wings to people's houses. Odd about my own house, though. Daniel bought it for us, wanted us nearby in the summers. I never did feel like launching a full-scale remodeling. I'm only happy doing that with other people's houses. It's the little things, the nooks and crannies, the piles of things everywhere, the backs of closets, forgotten stashes, that's what contents me. Do you like it here?

Very much.

You're a quiet fellow, Simeon. I don't talk well to you when we're alone. I don't know quite what to say. I should like you to spend a longer time here. Perhaps I might come to know you then.

There's the back door. It's Dan.

But it's an unlikely prospect. I'll have to trust you to yourself, a difficult thing for an overbearing old man. KNOCK THE SNOW OFF IN THE MUDROOM, DANIEL! DON'T COME TRUDGING IN HERE DRIPPING SNOW.

I hear Aunt Abby on the stairs.

(Aunt Abby, Dan)

Want to eat something before you go to bed?

I'm waiting for Sim to get out of the bathroom. I'll have another cookie. Uncle Tobe's gone up?

He's always in bed before me. He's asleep first, and up first. We have our routine. Have a little wine to put you to sleep?

Maybe a glass. I'm pretty sleepy already.

I'll go out and put the latch on the back door.

You don't have to lock up out in the country, do you?

I like to lock up at night. It ends the day. And Toby likes to open up in the morning. So cold in the mudroom. The wind's getting wild.

I had a great walk earlier.

You said.

I love wild wind. I always take a walk in the evening. I almost need it before I can go to sleep. No matter what the weather is, wherever I am I take walks.

I hope Toby's fire toasted up your nose and toes again. I can't bear getting into bed with cold toes. They never get warm.

Ten o'clock seems quite late out here. I'm pretty sleepy. Your old great-aunt can't last much beyond ten.

You were funny, Aunt Ab, ducking out of the way in those movies.

I don't know why Toby dug out those old movies. It's an awful thing to see yourself when young. I'd rather let the memory fade. You know how glad we are you two came to see us, Danny. We'll be talking you over for weeks. Hester's letters will have more substance now. And I can ask even more prying questions when I write her.

I'll write you too, Aunt Ab. I'll write you much more substantial letters than Ma does. I feel terrible I haven't written you for so long.

It's hard to keep writing substantial letters to a great-aunt and -uncle when you hardly see them. We don't expect you to.

But I want to. I've decided to pursue things like that, that matter to me.

Well, if you do write, Danny, you know how we'll enjoy it. We're so curious about you. And you know, you might write us something about this Miriam you've been so close to for so long. You've said practically nothing about her since you've been here. I haven't wanted to poke my nose in, and you seem to feel it's all over now, but she's been such a part of your life. I'd like to know about her. I'm curious, can't help myself. Why should the loves of the young matter to me at all, I wonder.

I haven't meant not to say anything about Mir. I don't know why I haven't.

I'd like to know what she's like, even if it hasn't come to anything between you. It'd help us to know you. You were close to her for so long, but I haven't got a sense of her, Danny, not of her, and I was hoping I would. All I know is that she teaches history at the community college, you said.

After she moved out, I thought about her all the time, kept talking about her. She was all I could talk about to my friends. I talked about her to Ma and Pa, trying to have them see what had happened. They didn't, blamed it on her, were just as glad for it, relieved. I finally let it drop. Then later I began to stop thinking about her myself, slowly. I put it off, she didn't come into my thoughts, and I didn't think about her at all. She didn't even come into my dreams, where you'd think she'd be. It's become impossible to think about her, for a month or two now. I've gone somewhat adrift, haven't paid attention to things. I think about memories far back, or tell myself the stories I used to tell myself when I was young. I don't think about Mir at all, except now and then coolly, at a great distance. It's become impossible to. Somehow I thought of driving out here when I lost my job and I knew Sim had vacation. I wanted the long drive out here with him, even if we said nothing much, sealed in the car, keeping quiet. I wanted to be with Sim for a time and be out here in these places again, first, before I could start thinking about Mir again. How can you stop thinking about someone you love? The way we were wondering at dinner about Hannah, has she stopped thinking about us?

Do write us about Mir, Danny. I feel you'd like to. Not if it makes you sad.

I'll always be sad about her, Aunt Ab. I won't meet anyone else I'll love as much. I can't imagine it. We were together over five years. It didn't seem like it would end. We had our routine. I'll always be sad, can't help it, if I think about her, if I don't. I wish you'd met her. You'd love her right away.

Write us what she was like.

I do want to write you and Uncle Tobe. I've decided to start doing things that matter to me.

And about Simmy too. He's certainly not going to write us. Tell us more than Hester does. Give us a feeling for Simmy, as he grows. Oh, Danny, by all means, do write. You know how we'll look forward to it. I'll answer faithfully, and I'll warn you, you should prepare for some outlandish responses from your old great-uncle. He can be rather hard to take in letters.

I'm used to Uncle Tobe.

He behaves as he does because he's a shy man. Can you tell that? When people come to visit, he goes off to the barn to putter.

You're both that way. You duck out of the way of the camera.

Two crackly old hermits, staying close to home. Here it is past ten, you see, and I can't even manage to last later in my own house. Listen to that wind. I hope it's going to be warm enough in the spare room. There are some old quilts in the chest under the window if you need them. I hope those beds are comfortable enough. They're a bit swaybacked. It's so musty in there and chilly.

We'll pile the quilts on. I won't have any trouble falling asleep. I'm half asleep now, more than half asleep. I'll wash out this glass. Can I unload the dishwasher?

Already done. I'll get the last of the lights. You find your way to bed first. I don't want you stumbling over something in the dark. I can get about this house in complete darkness myself as if I were blind.

(Sim, Dan)

That you?

In bed already?

Tell me when you're going to turn on the light.

Don't need a light.

I'm through in the bathroom.

I just went.

Did I fall asleep already?

I don't know.

Must have.

Do we need the extra quilts?

Are there extra quilts?

Aunt Ab said so, in the chest under the window.

I could use one.

I'll get them.

Do you need to turn on the light? I'll put my head under the pillow.

No, I can see. There's moonlight.

Close the curtains too, Dan. I forgot to.

It's still windy out.

I can hear it.

Here, I'll put a quilt over you. Should I tuck it in?

Thanks. Are you sleepy?

I'm very sleepy.

I can't tell if I fell asleep already. I'm sort of restless.

I like sleeping with wind in the trees. These beds are swaybacked all right, not good for sleeping on your stomach.

I sleep on my back. It's not too bad.

I always sleep on my stomach. I'll do without a pillow, that makes it better. Want an extra pillow?

I'll take an extra pillow. Toss it over. I like a pillow by my side. I have to be in a certain position or I can't fall asleep.

I'm more of a sprawler.

You didn't close the curtain, Dan.

Oh hell.

I'll get up and do it.

No, I'll do it, I forgot.

I'm up already. The floor's cold. My toes are really cold.

You sleep in just your underpants, Sim? I can see you at the window.

I can't stand pajamas. I get tangled. My toes!

I always sleep in pajamas. Don't you get cold?

I put enough covers on.

We've probably never slept in the same room before. I don't remember ever sleeping in the same room, do you? Trading off sleeping in the car doesn't count.

I don't remember sleeping in the same room.

Are you a snorer?

I don't know. I usually have to get up to go to the bathroom in the middle of the night though.

I sleep right through. I sprawl around and don't notice anything. Mir could push me off the bed and I wouldn't notice. I'm very sleepy.

Good night.

Are you sleepy enough to go to sleep?

I suppose.

I could keep talking even though I'm sleepy if you feel like talking some more.

No, I'm talked out. I'll fall asleep.

Well, sleep well.

You too.

What are you doing, Sim?

Tucking the quilt back in.

Dan's Dreams

I'm lying on the flat bottom of the boat, lying on my stomach, keeping warm. It tilts from side to side gently. I don't roll to one side or the other because I'm on my stomach with my arms and legs stretched out. It's a fountain boat meant for floating on the most landlocked fountain in the world. Whole tribes are bobbing up out of it, babies with wrinkled faces. They are netted and shaken out on the sand. They walk away, some east, some west. I do not see this. I know it is going on, but the boat floats over the fountain flatly, rocking. I lie flat, can't see up over the edges of it.

Pa walks about the fountain with a long pole with a shallow net at the end, dips it under the floating dead bees and scoops them up, shakes them on the grass along with rotting crab apples and dead leaves. Aunt Maddy's son is playing in the grass, the garden is around us, bees humming around the flowers, the monks tend the garden. I am small on the bottom of the boat, the wood is pitted, rotting, water seeping in. I lie here for hours as the water seeps, and the sun shines on me, the cool water creeps up my sides and tickles. Pa scoops out the bobbing wrinkled crab apples, the dead bees, skims the scum off the top of the pool. Maddy's son plays with the shaken-out crab apples in the grass, rolls them in his fingers. He is being shot at from the garage roof. The BBs miss his ears. Pa scoops and skims.

The wading pool makes waves as it contracts and expands. It is a breathing hole. It gets very wide and flat. Its edges are off in the distance, a line of mountains, then the edges come rushing in, contracting, the waves rush to the center, a whirlpool, the boat is whipped around in it. I lie flat, very small, as it planes up the whirlpool's sides, almost overturning, rushing around in wide circles. There are grips for my hands, my feet are in stirrups. Babies are bobbing up out of the whirling deep fountain, shooting into the air, in all directions, just missing me. They're tossed up onto the sand, brush themselves off and set out over the desert dunes. I'm present at the birth of these new migratory tribes. The wading pool expands and contracts. Now it expands, and its shores push out to the distance, the waters go down, the surface is glassy, it's only inches deep.

The boat is old and leaky. The water seeps in. It's up to my armpits and tickling. The whole thing is dragged out and hung up on the wall and I hang on to the grips. My wrists hurt. I keep my feet in the stirrups, hang there on the wall, pretend it's a torture device. I can get off it anytime. It's to scare Aunt Maddy. She's easily scared by the games we play. Don't do anything dangerous, don't make too much noise, the baby's playing in the courtyard, leave him alone, he's seven years younger than you are. Aunt Maddy's being very unfriendly to me. It's the way she always wanted to be able to be to me, but she had to be nice because she was my favorite aunt, but I've driven her too far, she's not going to make allowances anymore. Maddy's son is crawling about in the grass with his monkeys, little creatures squirming about. He likes to play with them. They're disgusting squirmy little things with eight legs covered with wet fur, little toothy smiles. He keeps picking them up and playing with them and setting them down, then they walk off in all directions and he picks one up, then another, confuses it, sets it down in another place. It scampers around in circles. I won't let him bring his monkeys over to where I'm play-ing. We call him Madison because he's Maddy's son. Hannah goes along with whatever I tell her. Madison, Madison, she keeps yelling at him. Hannah, stop calling him that. Ma will know I'm the one who thought it up.

My wrists hurt hanging on the boat. I believe I haven't any pajamas on, but I can't look down because my face is flat down against the crumbling, rotting bottom of the boat. BBs are just missing my bottom. They are shooting from the garage roof. I decide I have to get down. It's perfectly easy, I could have done it earlier. I run fast across the courtyard and into the house, up the stairs to the costume trunk. Gramma's coming down the hall. I can hear her. I have to get dressed before she sees me. Can she tell I don't have anything on underneath these robes and capes? I keep wrap-ping them around me.

The door's open leaving a rectangle of light on the wall. I tiptoe in and Simmy's sleeping. I can see him with covers pulled up almost over him, his nose peeking out a breathing hole. The covers hang down the side of the bed loosely, so I tuck them in. I want to kiss him good night, but he's all covered up and I wouldn't really want to kiss him on his snuffly nose. He has a cold as usual. I kneel beside the bed and reach my arm over him as he sleeps. I feel close to him. I'm sleepy too. I fall back asleep. I'd been awake, but now I fall back asleep. Good night, Simmy.

♦

I'm on the longest boat in the world. It cuts noiselessly through the water along a mountainous coast, thousands of families on its decks or looking from its portholes, carrying them to our farthest northern outpost, the edge of the unexplored territory, beyond which it's only snow.

I'm quite a different person, which pleases me. I'm politely addressed as Jock, but I'm not exactly he. I'm relieved to have got away from the Poore family, which I came on board with, Gramma and all. Now I'm looking for the family I belong to, but I don't expect to recognize them because I've never seen them before. I don't mind. I stop at an empty railing and lean over. I can see the mainland we are leaving behind, its snowy peaks. There is some fear among the passengers that we're reaching Russian waters. We're all given slips of paper that teach us to say Mir i Druzhba in case we meet any Russians.

Stalin is on the deck of the Russian ship. I can see it in the distance. It gets bigger as it approaches us, but it can't be as long as ours. Stalin is a little speck on board in a heavy military coat with a red star on his hat. I can see it even though he is a mere speck. All the families on board start to shout the words they've learned. There's no danger of collision though we are gliding by within inches of the Russian ship. Stalin smiles under his mustache and for a moment I am close enough to reach over and touch his nose, but I wouldn't really want to. I believe he catches my eye, twinkles at me the way Stalin can do. The corners of his lips turn up under his mustache. We have understood each other. I keep looking back as he gets smaller and smaller, only a speck in the distance.

It's cold on deck. I go down to the Great Hall. There's a concert. Each of the families has to perform. It's the Poores' turn. Everyone is waiting for Uncle Toby's grand entrance. The audience applauds when they catch sight of his white hair. He stands by the piano and bows, then sits down, spends some time adjusting the seat, wiping his hands with a handkerchief. I hope he doesn't start to play. I hope it's one of his jokes, that he'll slam down the lid and say: I'm not in the mood! But he starts playing beautifully, and there's Ma up there playing the violin, and Aunt Abby playing the viola, and old Aunt Mary, whom I haven't seen since she died, is playing a huge cello. They're wearing long gray robes and they sway from side to side, sawing away at their strings which are all connected to each other. The strings of the violin go over to the viola and then over to the cello and back to the violin. Pa is bored, Hannah has already left, she couldn't stand it anymore, and Simmy's asleep beside me. He's always falling asleep. He sleeps through everything. I hold him closer and he snuffles and snores out his breathing hole. I feel sleepy myself.

♦

The sail in the distance is Simmy's boat. He's out in it alone. He's always out in it. Whenever I come here for a weekend in the summer he's out in his sailboat. I can't stay long. I have to get back to Mir. She won't come down here. I don't blame her. Ma and Pa are as glad she won't. Simmy won't come in from sailing. It's late in the year to go sailing, too cold a wind, the water's too cold, it's time for dinner. Ma keeps coming and going from the kitchen, doesn't want to miss the conversation. It's not that we don't like Mir, Pa is saying, but we don't think you're resourceful enough for her. We think Mir is going to have to find herself a more resourceful person, not like you. We've known all along she would move out. We're very sensitive to these things, your Ma and I. What did I miss? says Ma, coming in from the kitchen.

Edna's out there rolling cookie dough. I come in in my bathrobe and sit down and listen to her talk about how the man on the radio say they going drop another bum in the desert. Lord, please don't let them drop no more bums, please don't let that old Staleen make no war for my boy when he grow up, I pray there won't be no war for my Danny. Why do they have to commence dropping them bums? They don't know what they doing, poor things, they think they know, but they don't know.

I pick at the dough and don't pay attention to Edna. She always talks like that. She stands at the sink. She's so short she can barely reach up and over it. She's humming a mournful song of hers, one of her moaning strange songs, all off-key, a song of my childhood, I recognize it, not a song to fall asleep to, much too strange and sad. I pretend I'm asleep until she stops and waddles out of the room, and then when she's gone I can fall asleep. I pull the covers around me. She's gone. I can't fall asleep when she's there, she has to go, move out, leave, then I can sleep.

♦

The strait is frozen, and everything is frozen from here north. We're wrapped in robes. The Eskimos sing as they drive the sled. It's a long drive, crossing the Asian continent from the eastern shore, down through the snowfields to the sheltered valley. We must drive fast. We have little time to make it. We have been told that preparations are being made for the coronation. On the high bluff ahead, rising above lesser towers, above the flags, is the highest tower of the king's own castle, and as we sail up the river and pull ashore at the dock and set first foot on Tannu Tuvan soil, we're pulled into the coronation crowds, bounced along through the twisty streets in a dance. I'm given a red flag. I lose Hannah. She has a gold flag. I see it disappear in a crowd going one way as I'm jostled off in another. Horns are blowing, everyone has bells on, and we're following drummers. Where's Hannah? This is one of our B and K Club games. The object is to contact Staleen and pass to him the secrets of the bum. We've obtained them from Eisenhower and Nixon who think we're working for them, but they're easily fooled by spies.

Now we're entering the palace square, and flags of all colors are flapping. I can never find Hannah. I become aware of the meaning of the dancing. From all the back alleys, through all the archways and passageways, one after another, streams of people with horns and drums and bells dance in front of the palace, representing in reverse the emigration of the tribes. They come from west and east, emerging in streams, at different moments, flowing into the square, greeted by the crowd's roar. They're returning, they're dancing home, in and out of each other, looping over and under in wiggling lines. I catch only glimpses of the walls and of the leaders of the world standing up on the crenellated battlements, come to honor the King on his coronation day. I see Staleen himself, in his heavy coat, his hat with the red star, his mustache. I see his smile. I understand it. He catches my eye as I whirl past. I have to convey the secrets of the bum. I break from my dancing line and dance, waving my flag, to the foot of the battlement. I can barely reach up and over and place the secret into his big hand. His eyes twinkle at me, and I know he understands me, and I'm whirled off in the dancing. I'll never see him again. He'll die soon, the friend of Tannu Tuva, the friend of peace, the friend.

I have to find Hannah. We can't stay to see the King. We have to escape before American spies find us out. Anyone we meet in a back alley may be an assassin. I find a small doorway and squeeze through. Hannah is coming toward me down the passageway. I got to Stalin, I say. I didn't have a chance, she says. Well, Hannah, one of us got there. That's why there were two of us, one or the other would be able to do the job. This relieves her. We always do things together. We're very close for a brother and sister. Now we have to get back to the river. We run down an alley. An assassin in a robe lurks under an archway. We rush by him. When we get to the dock, a mountain warlord is standing there, and his men are searching our boat. He yells at us that we're under arrest as Americans. I explain we're working for Staleen. He clamps handcuffs around our wrists, calls us enemy, marches us through twisty back streets, his men guarding us on either side. Edna warned us this would happen. A dancing crowd comes toward us in the narrow alley, waving flags. We're flattened against the wall as they dance past. The coronation has taken place, and now everyone will go get drunk. We're led through an archway, a heavy door shuts behind us. It's dark now. Hannah's been taken away from me, dragged off in the dark. We're far away now from the drums and horns and bells. There's a hollow sound, an echoing, I'm drunk, where am I?

In the dark, chained on a wall, my ankles in stirrups, my hands holding on to grips. The moist cold wall of the castle keep is behind me. I can't tell how far down the floor is. Where's Hannah? If I let go of the grips I'll fall. There's a dripping sound. I'll fall into a pool. It connects deep down with underground ducts, the water keeps springing from deep wells. I'm so sleepy from the wine. I mustn't fall asleep. I'll fall into the pool if I fall asleep. I'll sink into the passageways, the ducts, where's Hannah, in this darkness, what?

I'm awake. I'm having uncomfortable dreams, drowning dreams? Sim's snuffling. Maybe he's awake. It's cold, it's very early in the morning. I'm going back to sleep. Don't let myself get too awake, turn over, oof.

◆

Ma is sewing by the fire. It's late in the afternoon, autumn, brisk outside. Pa's out in the garage building something. I didn't want to go help him. I wouldn't know how. He's very perfectionist about his projects. Nails have to be exactly straight, things have to be level and plumb. So I came in by the fire with a book. Ma is there sewing. She has a record on. I'm pleased to find it's Mahler. If Ma plays it now it's because she knows how I used to love it. She understood me then. She doesn't now, doesn't know why she doesn't, but her intention to play something she knows I loved pleases me and makes me sad. I'm aware of a complicated emotion. I can't explain it. It passes as soon as I'm aware of it.

She sits sewing. The room is darkish, but there's a fire. The red setting sun comes in the window at a low angle. Redness flows over the books on the shelves by the fireplace. Ma's sewing robes for Gramma's seventy-eighth birthday using long thick gray thread, which she pulls out at arm's length then snips off with her shears. We are peaceful. The music makes us so. I think that Mir is sitting by the fire too, but she isn't. I have glimpses of her when I start to close my eyes, but she is never there when I look straight at her. I feel that Ma likes Mir despite herself, is trying to, finds herself surprisingly able to. This delights her, gives her something unexpected. Finally they have gotten used to each other. I'm used to them together. It has taken time for this to happen. It has happened without my noticing it.

Nonetheless I'm sad. That complicated emotion comes back. I can almost describe it. I will be able to remember it when I wake up. I'm sleeping now and will not remember unless I make it clear to myself now, but I can't quite make it clear. I can't explain it. It passes again. The firelight flows onto the hearth, the sunset flows over the red books and their gold lettering. I see the biography of Timothy Usk, the very book I've always wanted to read. I'll have to take it down from the shelf, push the secret button behind it that will open the passageway, but I'm too tired to get up.

The fireplace is hollowed out of the trunk of a big tree. The tree grows right up through the roof of the house. I can imagine its tall branches whipping about in the wind high above the roof. It's Simmy's tree. He plays in it all day and won't come down. It's the place he runs off to when you want to catch him. Up in the highest branches he sways back and forth. He pretends he's sailing out at sea. I would make him come down, but Ma doesn't mind him climbing up there, even in the wild wind and darkness. She's used to him out on his own.

I watch the fire in the tree trunk. It burns the big roots slowly and turns them to ash. The ashes are piling up in the room. Ma uses them to dye her yarn gray. It's raining outside. Branches tap the window. This being home in the wild wind is saddening. The music has turned stormy. I don't recognize it now. Ma tells me it is Usk. I've always wanted to hear one of his pieces. At last I'm hearing one, on a record, a real orchestra playing the music I only dreamed, but I can't concentrate on it because I'm so sad. I miss some of it. I may not have a chance to hear it again.

The sun is just at the horizon. I'm staring at it out the wet windowpane through the darkness. It's the label of an old seventy-eight, dark red with a gold edge. It's spinning, the sky around it black like a record. I stare at it through the windowpane. I can't focus on the gold lettering because it spins so fast, but I know what the record must be. I haven't heard it since Peter Whoaboat used to sing it in his crackly old voice. It's just at the horizon. It's beginning to slip under. The black sky around it whirls, and all the music of the world is cut in the sky's black grooves. This is the sunset record. Every evening it whirls, the music travels in the grooves, winding in, closer and closer to the dark red label, spinning halfway under the horizon. But I'm the one that's slipping away from it, not it from me. It's the earth turning under me, slipping me away, the record fixed there on its spindle. Now I can see only a bit of dark red, now only a bit of the gold edge, now only black. Now comes dusk.

When the phone rings I'm the one to get up and answer it. Ma sits sewing. Her yarn lies all around her in the gray ashes. She doesn't want to know who it is on the phone. She snips the yarn, as she winds it, with her shears. Why do you have to keep being so sad? says Pa to me over the phone. He's only out in the forge, but he's calling on the phone. You've been sad too long, he says. We don't understand, what else can we do? You don't do anything, you don't do anything, you're not resourceful, not resourceful, why don't you just start to cheer up? It's time for that. And then he starts to say it like a chant, at first friendly: Why don't you just cheer up? cheer up? cheer up? His voice changes each time he says it. It gets louder: Cheer up! Then angrier: Cheer up! Cheer up! Now it's a ghastly breathless gasp, but very loud: CHEER UP! There's a sudden gunshot at the other end of the phone. In the silence after it I hear the sound of a collapse. I know it's his body falling to the floor of the forge. I know that he's shot himself.

I'm awake. I know what I've just dreamt. What a thing to have dreamt. I'll get up. Where can I put on a light? I don't want to wake up Sim. I'll go pee. Where are my moccasins?

Sim's Dreams

The ball's rolling just ahead of me a little faster than I can keep running. It gets a little bit farther ahead. I keep trying to run faster but I can't. Now it's quite a bit ahead of me. I won't be able to catch up to it. Someone on the other team kicks it back in the other direction.

I'm having a hard time falling asleep.

The ball's rolling ahead of me. I can't run as fast as it rolls. It gets farther ahead. It's way ahead now on the other side of the field. There's no one else on the field. It stops rolling, so I keep running after it to kick it back. Who can I kick it back to? It's too dark to play. Everyone's gone home. I like to play soccer alone. I'm perfectly happy. I kick the ball and run after it. I run very fast and get ahead of it and kick it back in the other direction, but I intercept it and kick it back downfield. I run into the goal and dive on it to stop it just in time. I kick it out onto the field, run very fast, get under it, head the ball, it sails back toward the goal, but playing for the other team I run up to the ball, dance around it and get it away, then I take it right downfield, no one's there, and I slam it in the goal so fast I can't get there to stop it in time. One to nothing. Ma wants me to come in, but I don't want to. This is fun. I'm exhausted. I collapse on the field, just for a minute to catch my breath, but I fall asleep.

Why can't I fall asleep? I'm exhausted. I can hear Dan breathing. He's asleep. Why can't I fall asleep? I haven't slept well at all. I didn't really sleep in the car while Dan was driving. I'd sort of drift in and out, never asleep enough to have dreams. It makes me tense to hear Dan breathing in the other bed.

I'm playing soccer with Squinty. He's so drunk he's almost sick. He's not taking the game seriously. I kick the ball to him, and he laughs and jumps up to let it scoot under him. Oh, I musta missed, he says, and he laughs. He dances around laughing. I have to run past him and get the ball. I dribble it back in his direction. He runs up to stop me, keeps stumbling around trying to get the ball away from me. I'm good at confusing him. He trips over the ball and goes flat in the mud, laughing. I'll never get anywhere at this game,

Poore, he says. I kick the ball downfield. Hey, wait for me, yells Squinty. He has to keep squinting because the sun is shining right into his face. I come down the field fast, a big black shadow at him. He can hardly see me, and I make a goal. Two to nothing. It never was so good with Squinty before.

My elbow's fallen asleep. I'll try the other side. I seem to keep falling asleep, almost, not for long. How much time has passed? My toes are cold.

Mir's come to see my new apartment. I'm in bed naked under the covers. She's looking around the place, trying not to wake me up. The bed's in the alcove behind a curtain. She hasn't seen me yet. She pulls the curtain back: Oh, it's you, she says. I'm looking right at her. He didn't want me to come over here, she says. I'm sure he didn't, I say. She gets in bed beside me naked. He doesn't know about this, he doesn't even want me to be friends with you, she says. That's his problem, I say, playing along, but of course I'm scared. Mir is touching me. He might come in on us. She's fallen asleep on top of me, and I can't roll her off without waking her up. I'm not sleeping at all. I can't bear just lying here awake, not being able to move. The parts of me that aren't under her are cold, my toes, my nose. I can't pull the covers up. It would wake her. Even my breathing might wake her. I try to breathe as quietly as I can. She's sound asleep. What I'm afraid of is that he might come in. I've never met him, never seen him, she won't tell me anything about him. She says he's in England. I think he's found out about me and is going to come in here on us. Somehow he traced her. She's not very careful. He's already out in the other room rummaging around. I can hear him. I hear him open and close drawers, pick up things and put them down.

I'm lying on my back looking up through her hair falling over me. I see his arm reach in. There's bright light in the other room. He pulls back the curtain and stands there in a shadow looking down on us. I squint up at him. She keeps sleeping through all this. He just stands over us in a big black shadow. I can't tell who he is. He thinks we're making love, but we're not. I've been lying here trying to go to sleep. Maybe he understands. He doesn't do anything.

What was I dreaming? Me and Squinty? I've got a hard-on. I haven't beat off this whole trip. I don't usually go for so long without it. I wish Dan were in another room. I don't know if I can get to sleep without doing it, but I don't dare do it now, even very quietly. I could go into the bathroom, but I don't want to get up. It's too cold, it wouldn't be worth it. I can't get to sleep with my toes so cold. I keep thinking about them. I can't think of anything else. My toes are cold, my toes are cold. It makes me tense with Dan in the room. I'm afraid every noise I make might wake him up, even turning over in bed or rubbing my toes. I can't even blow my nose. Is he having his dreams now? They're supposed to come later at night, after you've been asleep for a while. Sometimes you have a few as you fall asleep, before your mind relaxes. I never remember any of mine. Even when I wake up and know I've just been having one, I still don't remember it.

♦

It's started snowing. Everything is bright outside. The woods are white. There is moonlight on the snow, and I've decided to go out tobogganing at night by myself. I carry the toboggan on my back through the deep snow. I keep sinking in and getting my feet wetter and colder, and the toboggan is heavy as snow falls and piles up on it. I could've come out with someone, but no one wanted to come. I'd rather be here by myself. I climb to the top of the hill and put the toboggan flat on the highest spot. The meadow is bright with snow in the moonlight. I sit down on the toboggan and hold the rope in each mitten, and I put my boots up against the curved prow, then I lean back, almost on my back, holding the rope. I nudge the toboggan with my bottom. It's stuck in the snow. I nudge it some more. I'm afraid it's not going to go, then it suddenly goes, very fast, off over the edge of the hill. It's a tremendously long hill, even though I'm going very fast I still have a long way to go on it. The snow's falling all around me, wet and cold, and the wind is whirling it in my face. When I finally get to the bottom I'm going so fast I start up the next hill and just make it to the top as I'm running out of speed, so I nudge myself over the top with my bottom, and I start down again. There's a whole range of hills I can go up and down, one after another. I can do this all night long. No one knows I'm out doing this. There's no one for miles. No one can hear me huffing as I nudge myself over the tops of hills and then yelling down the other sides. I want to make as much noise as I can. I don't care if I wake Dan up.

Now I'm slowing down, and I can't help rolling off the toboggan into the snow at the bottom of the gully and lying there laughing. Snow's falling around me, and of course I'm at the far end of the range of hills. I'll never be able to trudge back over them with the toboggan, and the slopes don't work the same way going back. You can't get going down and then be able to make it up the next, you have to walk. I can't get out of this gully. I'm not supposed to be down here. The steep hills rise up on each side. I'm supposed to be on top looking down, not down here. Dan doesn't want me here. I stand as still as I can. I might drown in snow standing here. There's no place I can go, and I can't get back. If Dan catches me here he'll be very mad, but he won't say anything. He'll leave me entirely alone.

The person who comes along is almost frozen. I can't tell who it is because his little face is puckered up with frost. Ice is hanging from his lips and nose. He speaks in gasps and keeps speaking as though he thinks I know what he's saying. The longer his icicles get, the shorter he gets. He holds his hand out to shake mine. He means to be friendly. I wonder whether I should shake it or not. I'm glad I have mittens on. I won't actually have to touch him. I put my right mitten out, but I pull my fingers in so he just shakes my empty mitten. His eyes stare icily at me when he realizes what I've done. He yells at me a word I don't understand. There is a hole in the snow. I follow him in, between huge icy rocks and into a dark space. All the brightness of the moon on the snow fades as we turn corners in the dark. And when a faint glow appears ahead, we steer for that. It turns out to be a rectangle of light high on a wall, a little window under an eave. And now he starts leaping about and dancing, laughing and laughing. I can only see shadows of his shape in front of me, between me and the window. There are moldy mattresses all around with other boys on them, but I can only hear them, imagine what they are doing, it's so dark, only an edge of the moon in the corner of the rectangle on the wall. Now there is more of it. It slides in full and hangs there shining on me in the middle of the room, and the light melts the snow off me. There are white puddles around me on the floor. People will think I've been beating off. My snowsuit has melted off too. I'm standing

naked in the light with a hard-on and white puddles around
me, and no one else is here. They've left, I'm alone. I feel
stupid for having done this. Now that it's over I feel so
stupid. What did I do it for? It wasn't worth it. Now what
am I going to do? I'm shivering here. Anyone might come
in. But the moon begins to pass beyond the rectangle. Now
only a corner of the rectangle is filled with it. When it goes
I'll be safe in complete darkness.

There is a dead body in here. As it died it got smaller,
week by week, half dead, three-quarters dead. I could see it.
Its face puckered up because there was too much skin for it.
It is somewhere in the dark here. It's scary spending the
night here in the cold and dark, but I wanted to. I wanted to
stay here one last time. Dan's asleep beside me in his sleeping bag now, in the dark. I lean over against him to know
he's there. Nothing wakes him up. This is a feeling I've
wanted with Dan. For a moment I have it. Then he rolls over
the other way, out of reach. I can't lean against him. I have
my pillow by my side and hold it as tight as I can pretending
it's not a pillow at all, and when I open my eyes and look up
at the ceiling, I see stars. I see a dark shadow drifting up out
of our dark room. It's Gramma's spirit leaving us, now that
she's dead. It's just a dark space. You can only tell it's there
because it blacks out a rectangle of stars as it drifts up to the
sky. When it gets there it bursts and scatters, and the star-
light brightens when it receives her.

Snow falls. I have my snowsuit on. I'm lying on my back
letting snow float down on me. It fills up the creases in my
snowsuit. I feel it around my ankles. Watery chunks of it
have got in under the elastic of my mittens.

I'm awake again. I can't fall asleep. This is a terrible night.
I was dreaming about snowstorms. Is it snowing again?

Now Dan's snoring. He's sound asleep. I can get up without waking him. I'm going to get up and see if it's snowing, peek out the curtain.

◆

Jake and Tom are playing army in the woods just beyond where I am. It's summer where they are, so I get up and go over there, and I take them two bottles of green pop. Jake snaps his out of my hand and says: What took you so long, you missed the fun, right, Tom? Tom's laughing, leaping around in the trees a little way off. You want a pop, Tom? I say. Tom comes dancing by and grabs the other bottle out of my hand and goes dancing off. Jake shakes up his bottle and squirts it at me, and Tom laughs. You don't ever have any fun, Simmy, Jake says. You don't fight back, you just tag along, you're boring to be with. I stare at him because I'm very mad, but I start to feel tears in my eyes. See that, he says, pointing to some big pearly drops strung on the blades of a square inch of grass. Know what that is? I say I don't know. You wouldn't know what that is, would you! he says. Tom knows, and he's younger than you are, he knows what that is. Tom is swinging on tree branches and laughing. I've seen a monkey do it in a zoo, I say. Do what? Jake says. Same thing you did, that stuff there. You never seen that in a zoo, says Jake. Yes I have. Then what is it? he says. I don't know what you call it, I say back.

We've got baby guns and we're on the garage roof peeking over into the courtyard. You shoot these things to kill babies, Jake says. There's one down there. Pang! he fires and ducks back down. Then Tom fires: Pang! Got him, he says, bloody little head. I'm not going to kill a baby, I say. You have to, Jake says. He squirts me in the face with the pop again. I start to hit at him with my fists, but he pushes me on my back. I fall on the gravelly roof and skid on my elbows. I'm worried about broken pop bottles smashed all over the roof. Jake keeps smashing them, and Tom thinks it's great. He's firing down into the garden: Pang! Pang! Pang! The baby's screeching, but it's still alive. I start to run away. Jake and Tom take off after me into the courtyard. I fall into the wading pool. They come splashing after me. I get out the other side, head for the woods. I run with them panging their guns after me, over my head. This is just a game, they yell. Then I only hear one set of footsteps. I know these woods so well I can escape. It's Dan behind me, we're running into the house. I got here first! I yell. I start tickling him. He starts to fight back. He gets hard all over, grabs my knees, tries to pick me up, tosses me over his head, but I'm strong. I hold on and get him to the floor. We tumble all over. It's not a fair match, but we're doing it for fun, but also because I've been mad at him all day. He drives me crazy sometimes. I'd like to smash him. I can't get away from him. He's always there. It's good to fight him. I smash him back down onto the floor because I'm stronger than he thought. He's laughing but he's fighting seriously too. You're a tough little brother, he says. I can tell he's been waiting for a time to let go at me like this. He's mad at me too. Now he gets me in the stomach. I'm more scared by this fight suddenly. I think he's very mad at me, would like to knock me out. I hate you so much, he keeps saying, smashing my face with his hands, you're so different from me and I can't stand it, smashing my face and making me bloody. He's on top of me, squashing me down on my back with his weight, and I'm holding on tightly to him trying to squeeze him till he stops. I hate you too, I'm not afraid to say it, but I can't reach him to bloody his face, his arms are longer. I fall on my back on the rug. He runs out of the room because Gramma's car has just driven in the driveway. She's coming for dinner. Pa tells us all to calm down. Ma comes downstairs. Edna comes out of the kitchen and tells me what a mess I am with Gramma coming. I look out the window. I can see the big black car in the driveway. It's sealed tight with Gramma in the back. We all go out the front door and down the steps to the car. I press against the window to see through the shiny pane. There's Gramma in the backseat in her fur coat, her hat, her pearl necklace, the car rug over her knees. Her skin is too large on her face. It hangs in wrinkles. She's much smaller than she was. Don't open the door, Pa says, it's sealed. You can look at her, but you can't touch her, she's dead. When you've had your last look, go back inside the house. Hannah's crying and runs back inside. Dan stares very seriously and then walks away gloomily into the backyard. I'm there alone looking in. The car rug slips off her knees. There's a wind in there. I'm afraid I'm going to see something I don't want to see, but I can't look away from the window. Her skirt begins to flutter. I don't want to see it. Pa's holding me by the shoulders making me look in. I can't get away. He's telling me how his little brother Jake at only nineteen was shot in the war and how he had to scatter his ashes himself in these woods, how Gramma couldn't bear it. Her skirt flutters. I see her dead knees, and then above them where her thighs start to decay, and as her skirt lifts in the wind I see her moldy lap and I can't tell what's what because it's all rotten and decayed, it has already begun to fade, the outlines of it, it's blurred, mildewed, the whole backseat of the car is rotting and Gramma's lap's part of it, the skirt flutters high over the molding pile. I can't see. It's becoming night, everything's darker.

I can't sleep. I keep waking up after nightmares. I don't remember them. I keep having them. Is the light on in the bathroom? Is Dan up? Dan's up. The light goes off. I hear him padding back in. I'll pretend to be asleep. Was I mad at him in a dream I just had? Why can't I remember my dreams? I never remember them, only a vague memory, which fades. Something about knees? Here he comes. He slips off his moccasins between the beds, he gets under the covers. He thinks I'm asleep. There's a faint light from behind the curtain, the beginning of morning. I'm wide awake. I won't go back to sleep. I often wake up early and can't get back to sleep, don't want to go back to sleep. I'll lie here and think only of watching the light grow behind the curtain, see if I can notice it growing, think only of it. It's grown already, since I've been watching. I'm aware of more of it, but I can still hardly tell it's there. Then in half an hour I'll get up and take a very hot bath before anyone else wakes up. Dan's already back to sleep. He breathes in regular gasps. He'll keep having new dreams while I watch the light. He remembers his dreams. Why don't I remember my dreams?

PART THREE

Conversation
(Jock, Dan)

Wait'll you see them. You've only seen Sam when he was just a blob, never seen Annie.

It'll be odd seeing your kids. It's going to be like seeing what I could've had now myself. And I haven't seen Mary since your trip three years ago. I hardly know Mary. She was pregnant with Annie then.

She'll be home by the time we get back. Has Sim met her? Well, they'll introduce themselves. Did he really want to stay there and sleep?

Sim sleeps a lot anyway. And he didn't sleep well last night. It's not been a calming trip, and we had to get up early today. It's a little stupid of us, cramming it all into five days.

I wish you'd stay more than one stupid day.

I know, I know, and I have nothing to get back to, but Sim does. Of course, I should get back too, start hunting for another job.

I thought maybe Sim figured he should stay at the house this afternoon since you're staying such a short time, so we could talk between ourselves. For a little brother he was always good about not getting in the way.

He often fades out after lunch, disappears into his room and sleeps when we're visiting Ma and Pa, or he falls asleep on the couch before dinner. He would've liked to have come with us, but I think he was really exhausted. Of course, he probably figured we wanted to talk too.

And we do want to talk, after all.

We do.

Remember Tannu Tuva, Dan? I remember you telling me how the king would ride through the city at the head of a vast regiment of camels on his coronation day. You'd go on as if you'd been there. Sometimes in high school we'd sit around and you'd go on and on about Tannu Tuva. Do you still have the maps you made and the histories? Remember that Tannu Tuvan language tape you made, like the ones we had in German class? You tried to get me to pronounce all those ceremonial words. Say something in Tannu Tuvan.

I've forgotten it all, haven't looked at any of that stuff for years.

I loved all that stuff, those beautiful maps. You'd come over and draw maps of Tannu Tuva while I was putting my amplifier together. I wish I had one of those maps to put on my wall. Send me one, I'll frame it and put it up. Send one that shows all the mountains and rivers with all those sensuous contour lines.

I'll see what I've got stashed away.

I don't have anything of yours, some photos, some letters somewhere, that's it. We should have some of each other's artifacts. I'll send you one of my graphs, pollution levels in the Rock River. It might even look sort of nice framed, despite the depressing statistics.

I'd love something like that. No, I actually would.

There's a sort of delicacy about graphs, patterns of thin

jagged lines, not as sensuous as your maps, more delicate, controlled. I've got some old graphs at home. You can pick the nicest. You know, Dan, by tomorrow it'll be cold and snowing again, I'll bet you, sweeping off the plains. Spend another night here with us, come on.

Sim's got to get back.

It'll snow. We won't be able to dig out. You'll be stuck here.

I should've gone out to the meadow. Why didn't I?

At your Gramma's?

Sim wanted to. It was deep snow. I thought I didn't want to. Where Tannu Tuva was, the gully. I should've trudged in there, sinking in the snow, getting wet and cold and not knowing exactly where I was, trying to figure out which part of the gully it was and stand over the place, not knowing what's still down there under the snow.

You should have.

I'd like to have stood there and felt I was there again. I'd like to have felt a bit sad about it. I didn't really feel sad in the house, the great hall, the chapel, the library. There hasn't been a moment when I've stopped to feel sad. My thoughts have been going too fast. I wanted to have one moment when it all came back to me from the past, when I recognized something I'd forgotten about. But all the Poore things are so familiar to me, I've never forgotten them. I lived with them too long, knew them too well, I dream of them still. Most of my dreams take place there. Why didn't I even want to trudge out to the meadow yesterday? Looking out from the top of the tower was all I wanted to do. It was all too familiar.

I remember being up there in the tower.

I'll bet you do, and Sarah does too, wherever she may be.

You're right. We needn't go into that.

Sim said he wanted to see the gully. We should've gone out there. Or I could've found the place where the old rotting boat was that Pa once planted with flowers. I'd like to have fallen down on the snow, something like that, stretched out in it thinking that I'm suspended by snow, suspended over the rotting old boat, that it's down there under me, rotting away under the snow, some such moment as that, when I might have felt sad, lain there with my arms and legs flung out in the snow letting flakes float down on me. And if there'd been a storm. I could have felt I was letting myself die in the snow, a feeling I could've had for a moment and then let pass, then gotten up and gone back. I want to have had some moment like that.

You used to write me complicated letters, Dan, up till last summer even, and then in the fall you wrote a short one or two, and after Christmas just the short one to say what had happened with Mir, and instead of answering when I wrote you back, after weeks you finally called and said, oh everything was under control, but you were coming out here with Sim on a last-minute trip. I didn't understand what had happened, still don't. I used to know all the complications of things all along from your letters, and from the trips I took east, even though I hardly knew Mir. But now your letters haven't said anything for so long. I suppose it must've been hard to account for in letters.

I couldn't explain it. I couldn't explain it on the phone either.

But what finally happened? How could you both have decided something like that after so long?

We hadn't changed much in the five years she was getting her degree. The various ups and downs didn't change us much. The things I used to write you were just ups and downs. But she was gradually getting panicked. We either had to take the next step or come to an end. I was the one who couldn't take the next step, not Mir. She wanted to have children, that's what it really was. She didn't want to wait any longer. I kept saying not quite yet. It begins to panic someone at her age when she's made up her mind at last. She didn't want to hold on a couple of years more and find I'm still saying not quite yet. She wanted to know it was going to be able to happen, not immediately necessarily, but soon. I don't know why I kept saying not quite yet. The thought of it panicked me. When you do something like that you don't undo it. It wasn't financial. She wasn't afraid of that. She has modest tastes, we're the same. She'd want me to have some steady job I liked, for my sake, but it wasn't a matter of a larger income. Ma and Pa don't understand that, but Mir and I were happy being slow paced. We'd have the time to be parents. We'd love it. I'd love it so much. But it's still me being unready for it. Driving up here this morning I was thinking. Sim was staring out the window. We weren't saying anything to each other. It was still early in the morning. I was thinking about the dreams I'd had. Well, I'd had a sort of nightmare in the middle of the night. I'd woken up in the middle of it, and then later after I'd been back asleep I dreamt about Aunt Abby and Uncle Toby. In my dream I didn't like the two of them at all. They were fussy and picky, they kept explaining to me how wonderful they were. That's terrible, they're my dear old aunt and uncle. It was a strange dream for me to have. When I woke up again, Sim was taking a bath. I lay in bed thinking about the dream. I don't remember exactly what happened in it. It was about going around locking up the house, some house

or other, and boarding up the windows and closing the flues
in the chimneys and covering the chairs and all these piled-
up old things, and Uncle Toby kept saying how he knew so
well what he had done with his life, he'd made the right
decisions, everything he'd done was wonderful, no one else
could've done things as well as he had, and Aunt Abby was
nodding and smiling. It was unpleasant. We'd had a good
conversation last night with them. I'd felt they were the best
of my whole family in a way, but I'd dreamt of them as so
self-centered and self-satisfied and unpleasant. At breakfast
I didn't feel as fond of them as I had the night before, as if
they were responsible for the way they'd appeared in my
dream. It was sad leaving. We hugged each other, and it does
seem possible I'll never see them again. It was sad. But then
driving along in the car I began to feel there really was
something I didn't like about them. Not about them, but
something about their hermit life made me mad at them.
And it's what I'd liked about them until the dream. In the
dream I didn't like it as much. And I didn't like how Uncle
Toby portrays himself as an old codger, doing it his own
way. He can talk as recklessly as he wants. What's he responsible for? This function he says he serves of keeping
people snappy! He was talking about who should have had
children and who shouldn't.

In the dream?

Last night at dinner. He was saying, well, he was putting
forth the thought, that Sim and Hannah and I probably
shouldn't have been born if all things had been thought out
properly. We were all a bit drunk, except Aunt Abby. In the
excitement discussing it all, I understood Uncle Toby. He
seemed to be lighting things up, saying the outlandish
things that had to be thought about. It made me think what

a great old man he was, a codger, of course, but great. I took a
walk after dark in the cold wind and thought to myself as I
walked along how wonderful he was, how that's the sort of
fresh-thinking way I admire. I mean, think of it, to contem-
plate your never having been born, that's thinking fresh! I
was striding along the back road down there through the
woods, almost singing to myself, a bit drunk, exhilarated. I
always take walks before bed to wear me out. Then I came
in and we all sat around the fire for a while, very much at
home, and talked, and I calmed down and felt sleepy. It
never occurred to me I'd wake up with such an opposite
feeling in the morning. Dreams can undo the whole day
before, things that have to be calmed down, put back, you
know?

But what about you and Mir, Dan?

Well, what Uncle Toby said about deciding to have children, or deciding not to.

I take it they decided not to, your uncle and aunt.

Decided, he kept making clear it had been decided, not
stumbled on. He said Sim and Hannah and I were stumbled
on. Sim's always thought he was a mistake, not even stumbled on, but actually not wanted. It turns out he's always
thought that.

Could it be?

It actually could. I hate to say it. I'd never thought of it,
but it wasn't as if Ma and Pa loved having little kids about
the place and would've wanted to keep them coming. I don't
have any idea why they had him.

When you said you'd love it, having kids about the place,
you would, I know you would, Dan, you especially. It's a
world of Tannu Tuvas, constantly, let me tell you. It's what I
love most about my life. Wait'll you see them.

Last night I felt Uncle Toby was telling me, see, your ma
and pa didn't want you enough to have been justified in
having you. And this morning I was feeling he had been
telling me I myself didn't want children enough to be justified in having them. He always intends things by what he
says, pokes around under the skin. You don't notice it at the
time. As if he were saying I was right to have backed off
from Mir, I don't have it in me. It's what he was saying about
the whole family, the flimsiness, the backing off. We've all
wanted to be self-sufficient, it's our tendency, trained to be,
well, you can even look at it financially. There's nothing we
can do to threaten our security, even by being secret Communists. Even if I gave everything away I couldn't know
what it'd be like to be in true danger, could always turn to
the family. We're self-sufficient, it's there. We could sit in
our playhouse of a castle and look out. We could go hide
there, draw ourselves in around us and hole up, never have
to come outside into the world. Everything there was our
own. Somehow Ma and Pa made the move east, to the sea,
started fresh, but it's the same thing, they're still hermits,
like Uncle Toby and Aunt Abby. And Hannah made the
move across the sea, but what do I ever hear from her, what
other people's lives does she think about? Where are her
children? And why did I tell Mir, keep telling her, I wasn't
quite ready? Am I putting it off forever? I don't do much of
anything. I've never really done anything. I've spent a lot of
time fiddling. I'm never bored. I've always been busy, but
what have I done? Here you are with your actual career. I
know what you meant when you were saying at lunch how
you do it though you don't have much hope for cleaning
things up, no one listens to what you say, in your little
realm, and there are all the other little realms, conflicting

interests, different analyses of the problem, and who's going to pay, how nothing can get done, it's too late anyway, all that, but you do it, you said, it gives you pleasure. It's not just making the money. There's always a new problem, your mind keeps going. But I don't think as much. I'm slowed down. I forget things. I don't listen to music as well as I did, seldom sit down with it and listen start to finish. It's true I'm not so romantic anymore. I don't expect those old feelings. I'm an orderly person, it suits me, but orderly people are supposed to work. No one in the family ever worked. When did I ever see anyone work? The money came in from mysterious sources, from what our grandfather had done years ago. There are times I think I should've studied cartography, me and my maps. Or economics, with my sixth-grade communism. Or I should've gone into linguistics, my Tannu Tuvan language, could've spent my life at it. Or music history, why not, a biographer of composers. I feel maybe I should go somewhere else now to start fresh, get away. Mir's not far away now, I see her, she isn't attached to anyone else, she feels miserable. Our old friends see both of us, tell us each how sad the other is, how hard it is for us both. Ma and Pa think it's her fault. They were actually glad to have her go. It was obvious in their polite way they couldn't bear her, the woman I really loved, still love, you can't stop loving when you've spent a long time learning how together. Sim was saying how he doesn't think they ever wanted him to love anyone. He believed them, he says, he believes he can't love, not only can't love a woman, a wife, but can't love at all, anyone, friends, it doesn't matter to me who it is if he only would try, he can't even be sure he loves me, his brother. We've been talking about it. I want to break through that. No, that's the wrong way to put it. I

have to stop thinking that way. It'll come from him. Why is
he so afraid? Of course I'm afraid too. I should know why
he's afraid. At times I don't believe I can love either. It
sweeps over me, I can't. I should know why Sim's afraid.
I've been through it. I'm coming out of it, and now he's
falling into the worst of it. I remember how it was, the
glumness you can't break through. I want to help him so
much, but he won't have help. He thinks he has to force
himself in a brutal way to do what he's terrified of and no
one else may help him. He doesn't know that the world
must be made of help, not all sorts of lies, like we know
you're good, we're on your side, you can do it, we have faith.
Maybe indeed you can't do it, maybe you're not good. Ma
and Pa fear that. They won't take a dilemma seriously,
admit the danger of it. They act as if there's no dilemma
because Ma and Pa are there, they're always going to love
you. But it's not love, it's hiding, holing up, in some silo
with gargoyle drainspouts looking out over woods and
fields that are all yours, no one else's, private land, private
places to hide. But how is it theirs? How can there be such a
thing as private land? How long ago was it the land of a
tribe? Not long, a hundred years, less than that, before our
grandfather bought it, and it had been fought over bloodily,
settled, bought up, sold, how fast it changed. And centuries
before the tribe it was bears' land. Now it's monks' land, and
they'll be on their way out too. The place should be set afire.
I felt like telling them when they were shuffling about
asking us how it was, young fellows, weekends at a country
estate like this, the implication being that we must've felt
so grand, rulers of the world, and I should've said it was
rotten, people should never be deluded to think such a place
could be theirs, if it exists at all it should be for all people. I

could've gone into one of my B and K Club harangues, started shouting slogans, pulled tapestries off the walls, smashed windows, smashed everything, this all has to come down, to all according to their needs, workers of the world unite, you have nothing to lose. In those very woods, Hannah and I would unfurl our Hammer and Sickle and wave it over our heads and shout at the tops of our voices, BUT YOUR CHAINS! And I meant it then, whatever crazy little kid I may have been, and I mean it still. I don't care what kind of a romantic I may be called for it, I don't care what kind of a hypocrite, me and my comfortable upbringing and academic tastes. I mean it despite all I may say and do, or not do, to the contrary. It's not for me anyway. It's for our children. It's something we only point toward, and it may even come. But of course it can't come because it will come too slowly. It's already too late. It's gone too far, the power's too great, the world's too large, the misery's too awful, death's too soon. I'm a completely unrealistic bum who can't keep his dumb job. From all according to their abilities! But at least I want to be able to love my brother. That's a step I can take. And next I want to be able to love my wife. That's the next step. I might have taken it. And then I want to be able to love my children, and I don't know if I can take steps beyond that. I don't even know if I can take those steps. I was close to them. Why did I say not quite yet? It's what they always say to revolutionaries, and I said it myself to Mir of all people. I'd begun to love her in a true way, you know, beyond the ways I'd tried to love before. The flimsiness had begun to fall away, the smoothed-over things. That's why I'm miserable about it. It was close to possible. And here I presume to help Sim. How good it would've been for him if Mir and I'd got married. It's awful for me to be

presuming to help him when I do nothing myself. He looks
at me and sees I don't do anything. He wishes I would shut
up, stop surrounding him with talk. He needs his distance.
Sim's always kept to the edges, woods, meadow, where he
could slip off. He liked to sail because he could get away
from everyone. I'm worried about Sim. We talked about this
business of not being able to love and he seems so resigned
to it. He wants to insist he has no sources of it inside. He
won't talk to me about any love affairs he's had. I guess he's
had some, brief ones, perhaps can't call them love affairs. I
don't even know if it's been with women, Jock. It doesn't
matter. I should probably tell him it doesn't matter. I suppose sex is for him still a self-centered thing. It takes a long
time to get beyond that if you haven't got beyond it at an
earlier age. Plenty of people are absentminded about sex, a
way of putting off. I'd begun to stop putting off with Mir,
and then I put her off and it seemed the end, the last putting
off. If I could decide to have children, if I could get back with
her, do you think I could do that? I torment myself with it. If
I could decide, if I could be with her again, I could decide,
it's something I could decide. I'm mad at Uncle Toby with
his damn decisions and his implications and his prods this
way and that, keeping people snappy, he says, sounding as if
I wasn't meant to have been born, not meant to have children of my own. He was warning me, with his hidden
meanings, his old mural in the tower room, those Norse
gods, remember? What the hell was all that about? He talks
about it as a private joke, his private gods, as if they meant
something to him. He considers himself a pagan, loves to
paint himself as an outlandish barbarian out of the hills
covered in bearskins, with a furious mustache, some sort of
Hun just off his camel from the steppes of Central Asia,

with his warrior gods, storming westward, plundering, rap-
ing, seizing land, building battlements, castles, giants fighting it out in the sky, he went on and on about it. I wanted
him to tell me last night. Today I'm sick of it, people's little
private mythologies, me and my Timothy Usk and my
Tannu Tuva, just as bad as Uncle Toby. Me playing down in
the gully in the meadow, driving toy cars along, Sim up on
the edge with his monkeys, a little presence, a brother
gnome, always there, wouldn't say anything. I liked him
being up there. We've been remembering so many little
things this past twenty-four hours, so many things we're
unsure of, memories, of the past, did it happen, were we that
small, did we know that little, did we think we were being
loved, what strange creatures did we turn to, what stories,
how far have we searched? Does he have to go through what
I went through? I can't do it for him. I want to spare him,
but still not spare him. I don't want to spare him, I want to
be near him while he goes through it, just near, so he knows
I'm there, all I can do, true help, the limits of it. He doesn't
have to tell me anything. It's sad, but I've gone through it,
still am going, maybe coming out of it, maybe not, I could
be deeper in it than before, he could be far ahead of me, I
can't presume, maybe I can make a decision, I can come
through it too, if he knows I'm his brother and want him
there, need him too, that's something he'll have to learn to
be responsible for because it scares him very much now,
being the same size, having to reciprocate, how to get out of
feeling it only as an obligation, his anger over it, how to
make his own decision because he wants it, not forced,
because he's himself, decide what he wants, dare to want it,
because he can have it, I will give it to him, and then there'll
be more who'll give it to him, some such creature for him as

Mir might be for me, might still be. For Sim who might such a creature be? Someone to sleep with the way he meant it, settled in, trusting, allowing him to sleep. He's too good for there not to be. He'll learn to sleep like that, it will be hard, I know, but he'll learn it, he will.

◆

We'll wait here, Dan. We'll surprise them because I usually pick them up down along the playground instead. They'll be out any minute. Prepare yourself for a barrage. They'll climb all over you, won't leave you alone. I'm afraid they may kill any thoughts you have about going back and getting Mir to have some kids with you after all. Just wait, they won't leave you alone. And then we'll get home, and Mary will be there, and Sim, and we'll all be roaring around for hours. I'm glad we got to talk. It won't be till late tonight we'll have that kind of peace again, letting yourself talk like that. Maybe I'll talk to you like that. It would be good. It's a thing there ought to be more time for. I'm going to convince you two to stay another day. Mary will too, she'll insist. And no more of this wishing you'd wandered off into the woods and pretended you were dying in the snow, please. Leave that place back there, let that be one place you don't see again, a place you came from once and don't remember, it's covered in deep snow. There ought to be one place in the world like that, one place you've been and will never be again. Oh, here they all come, pouring out of the doors. Where are my two?

Game
of
Spirit

◆

for John Korba

1

Lou had a hard time finding this place. No one knows him or where he is. He has not been here long. Where he sits the sun against the windowpane makes it almost warm. The sun fills the air, floods behind the walls, even up the stairs. Lou sees it in the crack under his door. His arms cross in the cold.

He has no furniture but black floorboards and a rug he brought last year from Mosquitia. It is prickly on the bottoms of his bare thighs. The sun approaches across the creatures on the rug, the pelicans, the coatimundis, the little boys. It approaches his toes.

Five telephone wires across the sky slightly quiver. Lou thinks of busting through the windowpane, walking straight out on the air. He thinks of hanging by his fingers from the telephone wires, naked, effortless, in a dream. Across the alley there are empty strings strung up from a window box for morning glories to climb. The loose ends flip the way his armpit hair would if he hung out there. What else moves? There is a faint breath in the sparse ailanthus tree with branches reaching up to the bottom of his window. A door flaps on loud hinges on a rooftop down the street. The sun is along his shins.

He thinks of the forest of Mosquitia and drinking all afternoon. Lou would watch the pelicans diving into the lagoon. One day the pet coatimundi on his rope hung himself from a tree. They had a hard time cutting him down. Come here he dead on tree! Lou was already on the path to his bungalow.

The sun is to his knees. He has no music in the silence but what is in his head. The five telephone wires like a stave of music quiver with the echo of a chord. Lou hears in the back of his head one note hanging a long time in the air. It stops. Silence in his head— Beside the lagoon he would drink all afternoon, the men all in white, his quiet guitar. And Lou, pulpy books under his arm in the morning, would walk along the sandy path to teach school. Once the little boys had left a pile of their shit on his desk.

Here it is not as hot yet, will never be. The sun on the tops of his thighs makes the hairs yellow not brown at that angle. Lou has been given an ID card by someone whose name is also, but spelled differently, Lew. He lives across the alley with the empty morning glory strings outside his window. Lou has use for the library to take out books with the card that is no use to Lew. Books from the library mostly about Central America are in three neat piles, due this week, due next week, due the next. A nice thing for this Lew to have done— He met him on the street. It is hard to think to sign the pink slip Lew not Lou. If he made a mistake, he could quickly crinkle the pink slip before the woman behind the desk saw it. Lew does not need his ID. Who is this Lew?

It is warm now up to his belly button. Black floorboards, dark green rug, the book piles— Pelicans, coatimundis, little boys are flooded in sun before him. They climb, perch in the trees, in the rug of trees, of trees behind these trees, which are only a surface. The sun makes him see almost into a forest. He waits to pick up and put on his thrown-about clothes till they are warm. The sun itself now comes into the windowpane. The five telephone wires disappear, it is so bright.

All rises now, all is warmer, all awake. The echo of a chord is gone. The sun is to each nipple, to his Adam's apple. It will not be as hot here as last year in Mosquitia. No one knows him yet. He hears the door flap on loud hinges down the street. A car passes. The sun fills the room, floods up to his lips, nose. His eyes close, sun against his eyelids. Now stand up. Silence, no thoughts in his head—

2

Lou, books due this week under his arm, comes down the stairs. On the second landing a brown-skinned little boy comes out a door. Little curlyhead, he is holding up an empty string and a detached yellow yo-yo.

"Put you me dis here froo?" he asks with an accent.

Lou stops on a stair. "Who are you?"

"Put you me dis here froo? Mama can it not right. I call me Niko."

Lou leaves his pile of books on a stair, takes the yo-yo and string and fiddles with them.

"Hanno say he have it not broke but he break it dat know I."

Lou listens to this funny talk from Niko with a cocked

head. He manages to get the string into a tiny slot inside the yo-yo and wind it back up.

"Fank you," says Niko and disappears behind the door.

"You kaka you kaka," Lou hears another little boy in there say.

He goes on down the stairs, books back under his arm, sweaty in his armpits now. These creaky stairs, these doors—

There is no sun in the library. It is air-conditioned. Lou signs the pink slip, careful to spell Lew. The young woman behind the desk knows him by now.

"Morning, Lew," she says.

"Morning, these are due"—and handing her the pink slip—"Could I get these?"

Lou waits at his favorite long mahogany table thinking of a cup of coffee soon. The woman behind the desk comes back with books due in three weeks.

She says, "Here you are, Lew."

Lou imagines Lou, then thinks of the woman, how she imagines Lew, and tries to think of himself as Lew. If someone called him Lou, the woman behind the desk could never tell the difference. Even if he met her on the street, so what if she said, "Hello, Lew." It sounds like Lou. No one would find out. What could happen? The books taken away, the ID taken away— It must not matter much to that Lew.

Back up the stairs, new books under his arm— Sitting on the stair now is another little boy, straighter hair but brown-skinned too. Lou remembers the name Hanno.

"Morning."

"Morgen," says Hanno.

"What language you speak?" asks Lou.

"English I can it good speak."

"I met your brother."

"Why have I such a bwuvva oh God!"

"I fixed his yo-yo for him. My name is Lou."

Hanno rolls his eyes and looks sick.

"Something wrong, Hanno?"

"What! Know you my name? Am I going cwazy? Oh God how like you such a bwuvva!"

"I don't have a brother myself," Lou says.

Hanno sits still, eyes down. "I tell you somefing what I fink. I have dis fing dat is always wif me always. Dis pawt of me dat is sometime inside me get de point?"

Lou looks hard at Hanno.

"Sometime is wight inside me exact same size in my skin. But sometime is wight next me wight beside." Hanno sticks his little arm out around nothing next to him. "I fink it is called my Spiwit."

Lou leans against the wall, the pile of books leans against his thigh, he cocks his head, looks at Hanno.

"Niko say de Spiwit not weal das ist blöde Phantasie."

"What language you speak?" Lou asks again.

"Papa in Amewican awmy. Lieutendon. He dead Jeep tip ova get de point?"

"Where you from?"

"Frankfurtz," Hanno says with a smirk.

Another door slams inside behind the door. Lou hears Niko yell, and another door slams.

"Oh God such a bwuvva I go shut up." Hanno gets up and leans against his door. "Stupid kaka!" he yells into it.

Lou has no key. Why have a key with no furniture? The long stairs up to his place— "See you, Hanno."

Doors slam.

3

He can tell nothing of this Lew across the alley. Behind the empty white strings he sees into his room. A shadow passes here and there. What does this Lew have? He has shelves full of books that Lou can see. A guitar lies sideways on one shelf. A cat sits on the windowsill. Lew never looks out his window. Only the familiar cat watches birds in the ailanthus tree. Lou had a cat himself, when he first came back from Mosquitia.

He lies on his rug reading. Most of the books are about Central America, if not the countries then, say, coatimundis, which lead him to other small mammals, or books about Spanish, which lead him to Spain. He does not remember much of what he reads. Alfonso XIII of Spain gave Mosquitia to Honduras in 1906, but fifty years later Nicaragua had not withdrawn its claim. He cannot find any information about the twenty-two years since. Who would want that swamp anyway, full of mosquitoes, coatimundis? He reads a book on swamps. That pile of their shit on his desk— He could only laugh, go sit and drink all that afternoon. And that coati swaying dead on the tree, the pet of the bar, they called him Kikatu. The pelicans diving in the lagoon, that lagoon that flooded Lou out— Honduras goes one way, Nicaragua the other, overlapping. You cannot tell on the map which owns Mosquitia, disputed territory, both countries at once.

He planted a garden, little rows of this and that. He tied up strings so vines could climb, tropical melons he did not know the names of. He had a little bungalow too close to the water. He thinks about the sand, lying on it at night finishing off a bottle. It could have been worse. Why did he come back here? This rug still, now in the middle of bare black floorboards, an island— He calls it Oblivia. Because he lies on it now in his clothes, it is prickly only on his elbows. He turns the pages.

Hanno said it is called the Spirit, something right beside him. He cannot say R. The Spirit is not real, said Niko. Who are those little boys? What language do they speak? Something Fonta Zee— Lou speaks only English. He does not speak to people often. No one knows him, not even that Lew.

The sun passes now beyond the rug island of Oblivia. He holds the book out on the floorboards to catch the sun before it edges up the wall and disappears. Lou will go out tonight. Here it will be all dark. There is no light bulb on the ceiling. His next purchase— The light comes on across the alley. A shadow passes behind the morning glory strings. Lou watches in the dark the shadow of the cat on the sill. The shadow of a man passes. Lew is there making dinner. Two shadows— Is it a woman too?

Lou stretches his arm out around nothing next to him. Fonta Zee?

Now he stands up to go out.

4

Niko is on the front stoop yo-yoing in the dark. Whip sprrr whip whap— Look out!

"Where you go?"

"Get a light bulb."

"Get you me cwackas?"

"What?"

"I say it right crrackas. Well Amerricans say crrackerrs."

"What kind? You have money, Niko?"

"I give you a quatta. No I say it right quarrterr. Dat's all. Hanno can it not right say de R."

Whip sprrr whap whap— Look out, Lou, step aside.

"Watch it with that yo-yo. What kind of crackers?"

"Sugar coat honey dip what is on Channel Sixty-six."

"I don't have a TV."

Hanno comes out on the stoop, slumps against the door and rolls his eyes. "In Frankfurtz we have Fernseh know what dat mean you dummy?" he says smirking.

"What language?"

"I can good English. In English Fernseh mean Faw See get de point? Mean you see faw even acwoss de sea. What! How you do dat? Fings in de sky."

"Hanno say faw he mean farr. He cannot de R."

"I can it so. Shut up."

Whip whip sprrr, look out, Hanno.

"You stupid kaka pipi get dat yo-yo fwom me out."

"Ha-ha!"

Lou says, "Hey, watch it, Niko, you'll hit somebody."

"You see de body he hit too," says Hanno pointing to himself in the belly button.

"He afrraid of yo-yo Hanno."

Whank! it hits him. Hanno slugs out at Niko, who jumps over the stoop, runs down the sidewalk. Look out, Hanno is right after him around the building.

A window pulls up on the second floor. What if Mama leans out? Lou gets out of there.

5

He has a box of crackers and two light bulbs in their corrugated package in his hand. He could not buy only one. Waiting in the eight-items-or-less line he flips through a magazine and stops at a picture of some star with the same name, Olivia, as someone he knew. She is hardly the same person. He puts the magazine back on the rack.

At another register the customer turns. He sees she is the young woman behind the desk at the library, gives two dollars to the woman at his register and gets two dimes and two pennies. Lou will give Niko the crackers but have eaten some of them. He almost forgot to buy them. Niko's quarter in his right pocket reminded him when he was in line the first time.

He leaves his aisle as the woman from the library leaves hers with two big bags.

"Hello, Lew," she says.

"Oh," says Lou, "I never saw you here before."

"I'm always running over," she says. "I live down the street."

"I live there," Lou says, remembering to point at the building Lew lives in, but she is not looking.

They are walking out. The door flips open on its own. There is a pile of free pink TV programs beside the door.

Lou thinks quickly. "I better get one of these," he says. He has never seen Lew's TV, but sometimes a bluish light shines from behind the empty strings late at night.

"You take a lot of books out," she says.

Being Lew, he cannot tell her all Lou's own books were burned last fall in a fire.

"Researching something?"

Lou knows this is a question she does not want a lengthy answer to. He nods and rolls his eyes the way Hanno did.

"I'm Judy," she says.

"I'm Lou," Lou says without thinking but realizes it is all right.

"I've seen enough of your pink slips to know you're Lew by now."

They are waiting for a lot of cars to pass. As soon as there is nothing from one direction a car comes from the other.

"Say, do you have a car?"

Lou almost says no, then he remembers Lew's car and nods.

Three weeks ago when he met Lew on the street he was getting into his new used car. He wanted to show it off to anyone and say what a deal he got at the government auction. The car still had INTERAGENCY MOTOR POOL stenciled on the doors. They talked, and Lou happened to mention how he'd lost all his books in a fire in his last apartment, and suddenly Lew offered him the ID. He closed the car door, rolled down the window and handed the green plastic card out to Lou. The car sputtered dead. "It takes awhile for this job to warm up, that's the only thing," Lew said turning the key again. "I've found a great Latin station at the end of the dial." A fast clanky Latin number came on. Lew tapped his fingers on the steering wheel and revved the engine. "I like the enforced wait," he said. "Keeps me from rushing off." Lou thanked him for the card and said he had to go.

Judy and he are on the other side of the street. "I'm looking for people with cars," she says. "Want to go to the

beach sometime? Look me up. It's the button marked SPREE,"
which she spells for him. "I live down there," she says
pointing at a building. "See you at the library."

When she goes off with her bags he decides to open the
crackers and eat some before Niko comes out. He tosses the
TV program in a trash can and holds the corrugated light-
bulb package lightly under his arm so he can tear open the
cracker box. They are honey-dipped instead of sugar-coated.

On the second landing he hears an angry woman's loud
voice speaking another language. He does not try to listen.
He leans the cracker box against the door and goes up the
stairs.

He manages to put in the light bulb in the dark. There is
that bluish light from Lew's window.

6

Because it is warmer he sleeps naked on his rug sometimes turning a bit up over him if he gets cold. His back is
stiff in the morning. Now that he has a light bulb he can
read late at night and needs a curtain to keep light out in the
early morning. This morning he sees little green stems
beginning to climb the strings outside Lew's window. While
the sun is still on that window he sees two pairs of naked
knees sticking up behind the sill, as if two people were on
their backs. Lew must have his bed there. The cat leaps onto
its sunny spot on the sill and flaps its tail as it settles.

A sudden bang on Lou's door— A little voice yells, "Fank
you faw cwackas. Well I mean forr crrackerrs. I fought you

have dem me no get. I go now in de school." Feet stomp away down the stairs. Lou has put his pants on in case he has to open the door. When he looks back at the window the knees are not there.

It makes him think back to the time he lost a whole house. He had lived with Olivia and some others, all of them long gone from here. It was on the other side of the city where the highway was not going through after all. Those duplex houses had gone cheap. Between the bunch of them they had bought it. It was a good deal because of the neighborhood, black people on one side, white on the other. No one lived in the other half of the duplex. The city had repossessed it, was going to tear it down, so they would have to make a new outside wall for their half, part of the deal. Olivia and he had on some mornings lain late in bed with their knees up in the sun like that. There was no one to look in but the empty space where the highway was never built.

How had he been able to live with people? He could sleep on either side of a bed and not get up and pee a couple of times at night from drinking. He could leave dirty dishes in the sink. They made a lot of noise because the other half of the house was empty. Who would complain?

If he knew Olivia now he would find out who she was by herself. She called herself Olivia then instead of Jean because she said it was more her own name. If she has gone back to Jean now— He thinks back wondering if he is in any part the same person either. He played the guitar then, he had a car.

He opens the window and lets the warm spring air in. If he goes to the library every day now and takes out books he will have several shelves full before he has to start taking them back. He could imagine them to be his own again, but he will have to get shelves. He might get talking to Judy each day a little more. That was not how he got to know Olivia.

Olivia and Lou and the rest had gone to their own families at Christmas. When they came back not only the other half of the house but their half as well had been plowed into the ground and nothing was there, no furniture, no rugs or curtains, nothing from their shelves. It was all under the ground in the filled-in cellar.

Lou came back first, and he saw a bulldozer with an address on it. When Olivia and the others came the bull-dozer was gone. They went to where Lou had written down it came from, but instead of that street number was a space of two feet between a Laundromat and a bar. Lou had also copied the bulldozer's license plate. The registry had an-other address for it, but it was not there either, and there was no such company in the phone book.

Olivia and Lou went again to look where their house had been. Some snow was unmelted in the shade of clumps of earth. Two-by-fours stuck up out of the ground. They knew what was underneath. But the rickety furniture had come with the house, the rugs had dog piss in them, and the curtains were yellow from unshaded sun. Lou had taken his guitar home with him, but Olivia had some favorite ear-rings and a necklace under there and an old pair of jeans ripped at the knees she did not want to lose. Still it was not so much to start again. It was more a good story than a disaster for them.

The city sent property tax bills to Lou's new address. He never paid, and after a while the city repossessed the disap-peared house. It was a mystery, but they did not need to solve it. Either the bulldozer figured both halves of the duplex were to go, or the city wanted the land and arranged for it. It was a bad neighborhood. Windows were always being broken. They would not have stayed there long or been able to sell the house anyway.

Lou did not live with Olivia again. He lived several other places. Then he signed up with the agency that said they would send him to Central America.

7

At the library Lou thinks of what he will say to Judy and begins to spell his own name on the pink slip. Whenever he crinkles those little pieces of paper he expects his cat, who used to hear that sound from anywhere, to come padding in wanting him to flip the little wad for her to chase, bring back and drop at his feet. Kikatu was not that kind of a pet. He sat on his branch or ran back and forth on it as far as his rope reached. He snarled at Lou with bared teeth when Lou tried to pat him. He was always there. Everyone who sat around the bar in the afternoon knew him.

"I'll send the boy for this monograph," says Judy. "It's in the subsubbasement. How's it going?"

Lou says the sorts of things you say. Someone he does not look at is in line behind him. He goes and waits at the long table. Because the weather is too good he goes out, when he gets his ten books, and walks a mile to the forest preserve at the city limits. He finds a place beside the canal.

The other Lew is spending the day there too. Lou did not

notice in the parking lot the olive green car with INTER-
AGENCY MOTOR POOL on its doors. It turns out the other Lew
has taken his army surplus inflatable raft and put it in the
canal at one end. He lies on his back with his knees up and
the back of his neck against the prow, looking up at the sky
and floating along. The canal pulls him slowly, winding
around, and if he hits the bank he pushes off with a bare
foot.

Lou would do that sort of thing if he had a raft. He does
not know the other Lew is on his way floating toward him.
He reads his books on the U.S. Marines in Nicaragua, or
Honduran mahogany exports, an illustrated book on mahogany furniture. Things come into his head, Alfonso XIII,
Fonta Zee, sometimes a bit of a song even. He might sing a
line or two out loud. You cannot escape the latest songs on
people's radios.

Lew is about to come around a bend in sight of Lou. His
olive green raft is the color of the water and hard to see, but
his yellow hair hanging over the prow catches the sun. Lou
is aware of something shiny on the water, but he does not at
first look up. As it goes by him he sees it is Lew.

"Hey, Lew?" he says just loud enough.

Lew's yellow head turns and then raises up and smiles.
"Hello, Lou. Hey, is this the life?"

"Not bad," says Lou.

On his back Lew must feel the sunlight against him
warm him through his shorts. It looks strongest around his
belly button. He has squashed a few mosquitoes on his skin.
He is trying to get sun on the undersides of his arms, the
palest parts. He is the sort to turn reddish.

He is drifting beyond Lou. "I got a six-pack in the cooler in
my car," he says. "I'll bring it round when I get to the

parking lot." The canal makes almost a loop through the forest preserve. Lew can come to a stop at one end and carry his raft on his head along the sandy path and start at the beginning by the parking lot.

"Sounds good," says Lou.

"See you, Lou." Lew passes under a footbridge. He looks up at the rotting boards with blue showing between them. Then he is out under the sun again. Lou hears him sing a faint song floating off. A Latin number?

Lou could use a beer. When Lew comes along the path, Lou hears the pshit of a tab being pulled. He looks around. Lew pulls the plastic from around the top of the open can and hands it to Lou. Then he pulls another out of the plastic and makes the pshit sound.

"I see you're making good use of my ID," he says looking at the ten books.

They have a conversation about ordinary sorts of things, nothing about who they are. How does this Lew get money, enough to buy those books on his shelves and that car, that raft? He never asks where Lou gets his money, but Lew tells him about his unemployment scheme and then about his draft card scheme.

He is a tricky character, it turns out. He makes investments with double the return. Last fall he hired himself. He called his company, which did not exist, FBN Piano Repair, his joke for Fly By Night, or more likely Nite. He never even fixed one broken string. He paid unemployment tax for himself for half a year, then he fired this employee he called Lewis Tennant, who just cannot get another job repairing pianos. Now Lew gets weekly checks and does what he wants, thinks up a new scheme for next year.

He has several names. In the days of the draft they did not

suspect you if you signed up for it. He signed up with different ages and names. With his draft cards he got other IDs. No wonder he did not mind lending Lou one.

In the afternoon they finish all the beer, Lew tosses the cans in the trees, and then they stop talking while Lew falls asleep for a bit on a mossy patch. When he wakes up he says, "Hey, I have my car here, want a ride back?"

Lou would rather stay here reading. He does not want to go home to his place where there is nothing to do any different from what he is doing here. He looks into the trees and hears cars behind them. This is not like the forest in Mosquitia. Beyond his bungalow it went on for miles and miles. He had no idea what it was filled with. He does hear birds here, a faint breeze, and Lew's car crunching gravel out of the parking lot.

8

Mama say I must you give two maw quattas well I mean quarrterrs." Niko is doing something with playing cards on the front stoop.

"No, Niko, it was a present."

"But my birfday is not yet."

"I ate some of them anyway."

"I give dem you." He hands Lou the quarters.

"What are you doing with the cards?"

"Well nuffing."

"I can show you a trick."

"Am vewy twicky twicky. I play on Hanno."

Lou lays out eight cards face up on the stoop in two contiguous quincunxes. One of the others in their half of the duplex played this trick on him once. Niko looks at him, chewing his fingernails.

"See this eight of spades?" says Lou. Niko nods. "See these eight spades on it? See how these eight cards are arranged?"

Niko's eyes puzzle over what Lou points at.

"See that this is like a map of that? The cards are laid out the same way the spades are on the eight."

"Dis is like dat. Dis is like dat."

"If I point to this spade in the lower left of the card, which big card does that mean?"

"I can it not."

"Which card is in the place this spade is?"

"I can it! Dis! Dis!" Niko points to the four of hearts in the lower left.

Lou explains how Hanno will point out a card while Niko is hiding his eyes. Then Lou will tap mysteriously on all the cards every which way, but Niko will only look at the eight. And wherever Lou taps the eight, on which spade, that will tell Niko which card Hanno picked.

"Twicky twicky," says Niko. "Always Hanno fink he know how fings go and it only stupid twick. I go get."

"Want to practice first?"

"No pwactice. I get Hanno." The door slams.

Hanno does not want to come down, and Niko runs back and says, "Mama say I come up now. I wememba me de twick. I pwactice. Well I mean prractice."

A week later Lou sees the little boys on the stoop. Hanno is rearranging the cards so his solitaire comes out right. Lou sits down beside him.

"Oh God not again you," says Hanno. He rolls his eyes.

"Hanno cheat wif carrds," says Niko watching him.

"What! How I cheat dummy? I not play wif somebody."

"Niko, do you want to show Hanno the trick?"

Hanno makes them wait till all his cards have fallen in the right piles. Lou tweaks Niko to distract him so Hanno can make readjustments.

"I win," says Hanno.

Niko scowls under his curly hair. Lou takes the cards and lays them out in the pattern of the eight.

"Close your eyes, Niko," he says. "Look away. Look at the Laundromat across the street. Now, Hanno, you point me out any card."

Hanno does not look trustfully at him. He points to the three of diamonds.

"Niko!" Niko's eyes fix on the eight.

Tip tip tap tip tap tap tip tip tip tip— Lou stops. He has pointed to the trick spade early on. Niko looks seriously at the cards.

"I fink it de red free."

Hanno looks mad and surprised. "What! How you do dat? I see you point at dem you point de wed fwee you cheat."

"Try again," says Lou.

Niko guesses the ten of clubs and the eight itself. Hanno is puzzling and twitching his foot on the concrete sidewalk.

"Why you have eight cawds? Put you ten cawds. I fix you."

"Sure, we can do it with ten," says Lou adding two cards and rearranging the pattern to correspond. He winks at Niko.

Niko yells, "I can de twick wif de ten no!"

"No, look, Niko, look, think," says Lou.

"I can de twick wif de ten no!" screams Niko. He swipes the cards with his hand all over the stoop and runs down the sidewalk and turns and pounds his fists on the bricks of the building.

"Such a bwuvva," says Hanno, "how like you dat?"

Niko stops pounding and disappears around the building. Should Lou go after him? He looks at Hanno.

"He always always twick me. I find dat not funny. Honey-dip him in de kaka."

Lou cannot help laughing. It pleases Hanno who smiles in a friendly way for once.

"Why you two fight so much?" asks Lou.

Hanno stares at Lou's eyes. "When you have bwuvva you get de point."

Lou leans back against the door. "Hanno, where is your spirit now?" he asks.

"You know somefing when Niko make dat twick I fink my Spiwit say I get out wight now. But I fink now it exact same size in my skin." He points at himself in the belly button.

Pounding around the corner of the building, Niko is running back and screaming, "Here come Kool-Aid!" He leaps up on the stoop and plops on the other side of Lou.

9

Lou carries a heavy old set of mahogany shelves. He runs into Lew washing the windows of his car with a blue squirt bottle and an old shammy.

"Lucky find," says Lou, "that alley behind your building, someone's trash pile."

"You can say one thing, I keep this bugger clean," Lew says.

Lou nods. He has nothing to say about a car. "Do you want your ID back?" he asks.

"Keep it as long as you want."

Lew gets in to do the windows from the inside. He turns up the Latin station. These are sounds Lou hears through the air from different directions when he is lying on his rug, pieces of songs depending on how the wind is blowing. It is hard to fall asleep now it is warm with windows open, cars and trucks downshifting and revving, burglar alarms going off by mistake. Men from the bar get into fights late at night then go off with their arms around each other.

"Want to have a beer on the corner?" asks Lew.

Lou takes his shelves up first. He comes down, and they go to Tod's and sit up at the bar. The motorcycles are not around at this hour. Lou and Lew order beers.

"Now I have this car," says Lew, "I feel like going someplace. To the mountains? Want to climb a mountain? Ever done it?"

"My family lives up there."

"We could go up for a day next week, climb an easy one. Getting to be weather for it. Like to be outdoors these days. Climb a mountain, float down the canal. Hey, go to the beach soon! Is that the life? You don't want to work all day all year long, hell! I suppose you have some sort of what they call a research grant."

This is a likely explanation of Lou, and he does not say no.

"Hey, this beer's dog piss," says Lew. "Why do I come in here? You like a friendly neighborhood bar? You get this joint."

"I wouldn't come in here after dark," Lou says.

"There was a shooting here," Lew says. "Before you moved in one night some slob comes running out firing shots at a bunch of guys he's chasing. Broke the windows in Mort's Market. They got the guy. He wasn't one of the bikers. Then there was the rubout a few years ago. Some slob was parked in front of the building next door, hey, that's yours, eating a sandwich, sitting in his front seat. I saw him when I walked past. As soon as I went inside, it must have been, the hit man pulls alongside and riddles him. A bullet through the glass of your front door— Ever notice it?"

"Some neighborhood," says Lou.

"Hey, no, this is high class, come on."

They order more beer. The other drinker at this hour is a lady with yellow-gray hair in strings and a cold face. She never looks at them.

"That's Dotty. Look out. She comes out and hits those bikers on the head with her broom when they rev up late at night."

"You live here long?" asks Lou.

"I've lived here awhile. But I come and go. Can't afford to give up my place, such a deal. I sublet if I'm taking off for a bit."

"You know those little boys on my front stoop, brown-skinned little boys, sort of half black?"

"Watched one play a sleazy game of solitaire once. They're new."

"You know someone named Judy, lives down the street, works at the library?"

Lew looks at him surprised. He takes a long swig. "I know who you mean probably."

"Met her at the market."

"You meet people slowly. You never know most of them. It's not a small town. You don't know who lives under you, wouldn't recognize them on the street. You make your own small town, a street corner here where you know someone, a third floor there, this bar but not that bar. I think of it that way. You have a small town spread out over the city in pieces, superimposed, you might say. A few streets you go on, this street, not that street, everything connected by telephone wires. I could draw a complicated map. Yours would be different, but they'd overlap. This street, Mort's Market, Tod's Bar, Judy—"

"How well you know her?"

"Not well."

"She thinks I'm you because of the ID at the library."

"I don't think she knows me by that name." Lew looks satisfied with his various names.

"Has she seen your car?"

"Doubt it."

"When she asked me I said I had a car because after all Lew does."

"She's always looking for a car to go someplace," says Lew. "She doesn't mind whose. Hey, you could borrow mine."

Lou does not want to feel he is taking advantage of this Lew. He has nothing to offer him.

"Don't worry about Judy," Lew says. "She has a good time."

They order third beers. The bartender is a man no one talks to. Lou forgets what he looks like until he looks at him.

Dotty starts talking loudly in the corner. "You don't catch me sitting around here drinking all afternoon. You wouldn't catch me dead in here. I wouldn't pay good money for this swill. I work hard all day and I have to come home to hoodlums roaring down my street breaking bottles on the sidewalk and beating on each other and those little colored boys screaming and yelling with their mother out whoring, you can bet. I saw it coming. You don't see me around this place. You wouldn't catch me dead here."

"Shut up, Dotty," says Tod without turning around washing glasses.

10

Judy did tell him to look her up. He looks for the button marked SPREE. It looks like the name has been clipped from a newspaper. She buzzes him in. He did not look at the number and does not know which floor to go to. He cannot go back to look without having to buzz again. He starts up the stairs. It is a big building with several apartments to a floor. The stairs are iron and marble, do not creak.

She is not standing in the hall on the second landing. He goes to the third. She is not there, so he goes on and hears a door open way above him, not on the fourth but the fifth. "You get your exercise," she calls down.

"You must," he says.

"I'm an old mountain climber," says Judy now in view. "You know what it's like on the third landing when something soaks through one of the bags you're carrying and the other starts to slip? The elevator worked once."

"Hi," says Lou.

"Hello, come in. I knew it was you. I was leaning out the window watching the street."

Judy has lots of things in her apartment that collapse or detach, nothing heavy to carry. The couch comes apart in pillows, the tables fold, nothing has thick legs. The travel posters of high mountain views and the white rug would roll up. The place could go in one load.

"My idea is to get it all into somebody's car and move. I'll probably be moving this summer."

Lou asks her where, but she does not know. He says he will stay where he is.

Her shelves are stacked plastic milk crates. "I won't have to go begging liquor boxes from bars when I move," she says. "Have a beer?"

Judy tells him when he asks that she has been working at the library longer than she wants to. First she was a shelf reader in the subsubbasement with the monographs and noncirculating periodicals. She liked it because she could think about anything. At the front desk she has to be friendly. She will not do this sort of work for her life but does not know what she would like.

"I'd like to sit in the sun on nice days. The sort of job where I could talk to people, not to be friendly— Have you ever worked behind a desk? You know what it's like when fifty people tell you something about the weather? You think you're going crazy."

Lou cannot help saying, "You fink you going cwazy." He explains, "It's how these little boys in my—these little boys in the building next door talk. They're always out on the stoop."

"Across the street from Tod's? Little black kids with a German mother? I talked to her in the market. She finally came over for the VA benefits. I didn't follow the story. Her husband was killed before the second kid was born."

Lou thinks to ask her, "How did you get your name on your doorbell in print like that?"

"From a headline: GUNMAN GOES ON SPREE. When my name shows up in print I clip it. Too bad you spell yours with two Ns. There's lots in the papers about tenants' unions."

Lou has to remember what she thinks his last name is. He sits on the pillow couch, she sits on an inflatable chair, they drink their beers.

"This fits in a small bag," she says, tapping the bouncy black plastic of her chair. "It's not bad to sit in."

"You like having these things that fold up or come apart," says Lou.

"My goal," Judy says, "is to have infinitely collapsible furniture that will all fit into my purse. The thinnest strongest plastic, the sort they develop for spaceflight—"

"The thing is not to own anything," Lou says.

"Not possible. But I want to be able to fold it all away. I have a hammock not a bed," she says pointing to the other room where something black is strung up. "It supports a quarter ton, and I can put it in my purse."

"You don't get a stiff back?"

"It's great, the air is all around me, I can slip into my nylon sleep sack or when it's colder my down bag. There's one thing it's not good for." She grins at Lou.

Lou cocks his head at her with his own grin.

"But I go to a friend's for that," she says. "He lives up the street. We've been a bit off and on lately. I'm going to be picky finding anyone else. I'm not in a rush."

"That's a good way to be," says Lou looking off a bit at one of the mountain views. He hears a door flap suddenly loudly above his head.

"And I'm also going to be picky finding a job, that's another thing," Judy says. "I'm not quite ready. I'm afraid of interviews. I wish I knew someone who could arrange something." She has finished the beer, which she sets on the white rug. When she leans back in her chair it flexes in the arms. "I'm sorry I don't have enough to ask you for dinner, Lew. Want to go out to get something?"

"I ate already. I just dropped in. I thought I'd see where you live."

"Maybe we could go to the beach sometime," Judy says. "I want to fly my kite." She points to the other room where Lou can see part of a bumblebee kite on the wall. "That'd be the thing," she says, "to be able to fly everything I own, everything light as it can possibly be. My hammock only weighs eight ounces, but it can support a quarter ton."

In a bit Judy says she has to make a phone call, but Lou says he has to go anyway, which he then does. They will see each other again.

11

Hot day, Hanno," says Lou on the stoop.

"Dat you can say ten times."

"Are you up to anything?"

"What say you? How I am up you dummy? I am down. Niko is up. Mama tell him stay inside get de point?"

"You're a joker, Hanno," says Lou.

"What is dat joka! I find dat not funny. Apropos I tell you somefing. You know what is de wind?"

"What is the wind?"

Hanno looks a little embarrassed to say. "De wind is God's fawt." He waits a second then says, "Get de point?"

"Fought?" says Lou. "Thought? The wind is God's thought? How metaphysical, Hanno."

"What what metaphysico aw you cwazy? Fawt! Fawt! De wind is God's fawt! Er macht ein kleines Fürzchen get de point you dummy?" His eyes roll.

"Fart!" says Lou too late to laugh, but he tries.

"You find dat not funny oh God. I make jokes no good. Dey always laugh laugh when Niko make de jokes kaka in de bwain."

"That was a good joke. It's your accent."

"What is dat accent?"

"Your German accent."

"What how know you dat? I can good English vewy smawt. Miss O'Weilly say I in special class. Sometime I shut up you."

"Don't get so mad," says Lou.

"Oh God not again I go up." But he does not get up from the stoop. He looks at his feet in their little smudgy sneakers, tapping them on the stoop.

The car from the Interagency Motor Pool passes, parks, and Lew gets out giving a wave. He slides a six-pack off the front seat and walks over to Lou.

"Lew, this is Hanno." Lew puts his hand out to Hanno's little hand. "Hanno, this is someone else named Lew."

"Not again," says Hanno.

Lew opens two cans and hands one to Lou. He sits on the step below Hanno and Lou, stretching his legs on the side-walk, elbows back on the top step.

"Too hot," Lew says. "Hot sidewalk. No wind at all."

Hanno perks up. "You know what is de wind?" he asks Lew.

"You want a scientific explanation?" asks Lew.

"It's a joke," Lou says.

"Shut up dummy you spoil." He turns to Lew. "How you not know what is de wind?"

"I give up," says Lew.

"De wind," says Hanno, "is how God make fawts."

Lew spurts into his beer, and his eyes open wide, he snorts his laugh. "Hey, where did you get this kid?" he asks Lou.

"Lew liked your joke, Hanno," Lou says.

Hanno is pleased. "Dat have I wif my bwain fought up." Lou pats Hanno's head on his straightish brown hair.

Lew thinks a minute. "I suppose you've got a similar explanation of rain?" he asks.

"And wain is God's pipi you dummy."

Lew is not so much laughing as interested. "Snow?" he asks.

"Dat is only fwozen pipi of God get de point?"

Lew leans back on one elbow with his mouth to the beer can. He looks up at Hanno. "Should I go on?" he asks Lou. Lou shrugs. "Okay, hey, what's God's shit?"

"Metaphysico," says Hanno.

Lew slaps his forehead and stares at this Hanno. "Who is this little bugger?"

"No no I tell you I tell you," Hanno almost yells in a sudden inspiration. "God's shits—what we say kaka"—he nods seriously—"you neva neva see it. Why you no see? Dat is what is gwound. God make kaka in de dawk so no one eva eva see. God is shy." Hanno looks up at Lou's and Lew's expressions to make sure they are listening. "Apropos I tell you somefing. De uff stawt when God make one little kaka."

"Uff?" wonders Lou.

"Earth," Lew guesses.

"Den he make maw kaka den maw kaka. Fousand and fousand time de uff get bigga bigga wif God's kaka. You find dat not funny?"

"Give this kid a beer," says Lew, opening another, but for himself.

"I tell you somefing," says Hanno. His voice is louder. He gets excited telling his story. "You know what is de fiah?"

"What is fire?" says Lew understanding the accent.

"De fiah is de stwangest stwangest of all what is God. Dat have Mama tell me." He makes sure they are listening. "Dat is how God love you wif de fiah," he says slowly. He looks at Lew. "Look what if you dwiving in dat caw? See dat caw? Dat can be you caw tip ova on de woad completely explode. You understand dummy? Den de fiah come all ova. Completely explode den you dead get de point? De mama say dat is when God love you so he love you in de fiah take you to see him you go away. Nuffing left what you say ashes."

"You lost me," says Lew who is more interested than Lou.

"De fiah is how God love you get de point?" says Hanno. "De only fing den is you Spiwit. De Spiwit always always wif you. Also you have a Spiwit. Yes you I tell you dat. You can it not see but I know it."

"Reassuring," says Lew with his beer.

Hanno would like a sip of beer, and Lew lets him have one. "Boing!" goes Hanno bugging his eyes.

"Good stuff?" asks Lew.

"Dat you can say ten times," Hanno says.

Lou thinks it was wrong of Hanno's mama to explain the exploding jeep as God's love that took away his papa, took him in the fire to see him because he loved him. Hanno could do with less of God's love in that case. Lou puts his hand on Hanno's soft hair and pats it again.

Hanno, thinking of the beer he just drank, suddenly goes "Boing!" again, eyes bugging out.

12

On his rug at night, his light bulb switched off, some light coming in from streetlamps— It is still hot. Across the alley in Lew's window the bluish light and shadows— Lou cannot tell what is what. There are black squiggles at the bottom of that window, the leaves of morning glories starting to climb. He will soon not be able to see the knees in the morning.

His own window is open. Songs from radios drift in and out of his ears. Cars pass coming from one side softly, getting loud, and fading off. Sometimes they cross. Yelling leaving Tod's Bar: I'm gonna fuckin' kill ya— He has heard this before. His bare skin is sweaty, but when a faint breeze comes in the warm sweat turns cold. He would pull up a side of his rug Oblivia around him, but he would get hot again. The breeze is infrequent.

There is the dark shape of his new shelves against the wall. He can see his books on them not filling them up but more so each day. The big book about Caribbean currents is on its side. Before he decides to fall asleep he will get up and hook his new green curtain over the window. He bought it at a rummage sale for a dollar.

In the dim light he can look at the rug and just see things, the eyes of a coatimundi in a tree, a pelican's yellow bill. He sees the faintest twinings of branches in branches, in darker and darker shadows of green. He presses his nose against the rug, spreads his arms out on it, stretches his legs. He feels it up and down him, prickly on his sweatiness.

In Mosquitia those months of heat when he could not cool off even in the lagoon— For all he drank he could not cool off. He expected to be always hot, forgot coolness. There was nothing to remember from his life before. He slept in his little bungalow in a hammock above the floor, mosquito netting around him. At night there were buzzings. Once through a rip a bat managed to fix itself to his heel. Outside there were howls and snarls and more buzzings and flappings. He never went beyond the beach at night. Even drunk he staggered home early.

He could hear the lagoon sometimes in a storm, but he was asleep when the flood came. He knew the water was high. He had not been able to sit on the beach to finish the bottle. He had climbed into his hammock and let the bottle fall to the floor when he was done.

In the middle of night he felt a coolness on his bottom through his pants. He did not sleep naked because people would peek at him through the glassless window at night, and he would hear them laughing. I have not wet my bed, he thought first waking up, for a moment thinking he was a little boy. In moonlight he saw his bottle floating a few inches from his eyes outside the netting. I will drown was his next thought. But he remembered he was not tied into his netting, it was not like a cage. The water was rising. The shelf on the wall with his few books suddenly splashed into the water. Now Lou was awake.

He ripped the netting, tangling himself, but then slipped out into the lagoon that was in his bungalow. There was the window that had no glass, its sill below the water. He could swim out it. Should he save anything? His guitar still high on the wall where he hung it—

With it held upside down by its neck above his head, paddling with the other hand, he was out the window on the huge moonlit lagoon. The storm had ended, and this flood had come suddenly afterwards. Now it was calm, and the water was not rising more. It was a long paddle over the depths of black water to higher ground. Some of the melons from his drowned garden bobbed up and floated alongside him and his guitar. From a tree on what was now the lagoon's shore there was laughing down at him and a couple of other people in white pants and shirts standing on the bank laughing at him. This was no real disaster. Even Lou laughed now that he was entirely awake and knew he was not dreaming.

Do I remember all that? he asks himself now on his rug, his remnant of Mosquitia. When he was leaving he bought the rug for a couple of dollars. This is how I can remember things, Lou thinks, with things to remind me. He stares into the darkness of green.

When he has gotten up to hook up his curtain and lain back down and almost fallen asleep and the outside sounds are quieter, he hears that door flapping on some roof down the street. He remembers what he did not notice then, the door flapping on the roof of Judy's building. There had been a loud slam while he was sitting there. She must now be hearing this same noise only much louder, and how can she sleep? Perhaps she is not in her hammock tonight, naked, suspended in air. This may be one of her nights out.

The noises downstairs have begun faintly. He has heard them on some nights late through the floorboards pressing his ear to them. He has no idea who lives in that apartment, the one behind the little boys and their mama. He has never passed anyone coming or going.

He hears faint gruntings and sighings. He flips back a corner of the rug and presses his ear to the floorboards. It never lasts long enough to get a good idea. Sometimes there are slapping sounds. The gruntings come steadily at the same deep pitch. Then the sighings quiver up and down, silent, then rising, then disappearing, then rising. They are not necessarily made by a woman. Once after a slap there was a loud low moan. Tonight it does not last long, a few grunts, a couple of sighs, low mumbly laughter.

With his curtain it is too dark to see anything in his room, shadows or patterns or the edge of the rug against the floor. He falls asleep soon enough. The door on Judy's roof flaps when the breeze picks up. Lou makes his own snoring noises into the night.

13

He sleeps later. The sun does not wake him touching his toes and edging up his body. He gets up to take down that curtain, lets it fall over him so he will not be naked at the window. He does not sit in the sun but finds the shady corner, wrapped in the curtain. He adjusts to day. He stares at the five telephone wires and thinks of something that was in a dream, but he does not remember it.

Oh, it was his guitar, when one string broke, and he had to leave it that way, retune it. He could not get a sixth string in Mosquitia. These telephone wires do not attach his building to Lew's. At the end of the block near Tod's there are subsidiary wires that do. If he had a phone his words would go along the wires across the city where they would get switched to Lew's line and come speeding back past his window to that pole near Tod's and slip into Lew's ear.

A buzz Lou has not heard before— It is his own doorbell, which he did not know he had. This is the day to climb a mountain with Lew, who said he would come by in the morning. Lou is up and jumping into clothes, socks, boots. Going down the stairs he is straightening his tangled pockets, zipping his fly, and only on the stoop where Lew is does he tie his flapping laces.

Lew is talking to Niko, who has a workbook under his arm. Lou opens the door with the bullet hole through the glass and hears, "Am vewy vewy smarrt, getting smarrter evewy day."

"This one's what I call confident," says Lew.

"Hanno hate it de school. He can it not good. Miss Forp fink I de best best in firrst grrade. Hanno in firrd but now he in special. He can only not wead well I mean rread. Dat's all. Tune in next week on Sixty-six." Niko takes off running down the block.

"Hey, Lou, want to climb a mountain?" says Lew. "I got a six-pack for afterwards in the cooler. After that kind of exercise it'll wipe us out."

The sun is bright on Lew's yellow hair. The olive green car is right in front. They get in and wait while it warms up. Lew watches the needle go from C halfway over to H while his Latin station plays and he taps on the steering wheel.

Lou watches Dotty in her pink slip bending over her little front garden putting in her tomato plants. "There's that Dotty," he says.

"That's where she lives," says Lew. "She was here before the neighborhood changed. She grew up in that house, the old drunk. She's the Laundromat attendant."

"How safe is it in this neighborhood?" asks Lou.

"You stay long enough you'll get broken into. If you have anything they can sell it'll go. They got my TV, came up the fire escape and broke the side window, so I told my insurance company they got my TV and also my FM, so now I have a nice big FM too and my premium only went up a little. It's what you have to do. It's easy to bust in. Had to do it once, locked myself out. I was on the sill, and I stepped on something soft, revolting, it was a bat. I had a six-pack in a brown bag, so I took it out and kicked the bat in the bag. Couldn't bring myself to step on it again out of mercy. I put the bag in the freezer so it could have a gentle unnoticed death. I completely forgot about that frozen bat. Hey, the weather said it was going to be clouding up in the mountains. Might not have much of a view."

"We'll get exercise whatever," Lou says.

"Look," says Lew pointing.

They watch the front door of Lou's building open slightly and Hanno slip out with a workbook in his hand. He has funny pink rubber gloves on. He does not see them in the car, walks just by them, eyes on sneakers, slumping, off to his special class, not third grade.

Lou likes hearing the music loud inside the car. It wakes him up.

14

On the road to the mountains Lew tells about Dotty and the bikers.

"She comes out one night with a broom. I could see from my side window." It is not the window of his Lou looks in. "Get the goddamn hell outa my neighborhood, you Nazis, she screams swinging the broom at them. They're the Fourth Reich with swastikas on their gas tanks. I'm loaded, so look out, she says. I saw you pissing on my tomato plants. Hey, cool it, old Dot, they say dodging her swipes."

"They have swastikas on their gas tanks?" asks Lou. "Do they have any idea?"

"They're not teenagers," Lew says. "They're in their thirties, big fuzzy guys with deep belly buttons hanging out. Stupid chains on their blue jean vests— What assholes! You stick your dick through my fence again, you'll be lucky to have a stub to piss with, she says. What a foul old dame. Aw, suck me off, Dot, says one of them. I wouldn't doubt he pulled it out for her. So she swipes at them and swipes at them. They're throwing bottles. It goes on every night in the summer. Glad you moved here?"

"My other neighborhood was the same," Lou says.

"Where you had your fire? Hey, you can say one thing, it's gonna be silent up this mountain. Look at it clouding up. No one'll be climbing."

They are in the country. Now it is not a divided highway, and the high-voltage wires interfere with the radio making it buzz. Lew finally switches off his faint station.

"Of course she goes drinking with them half the time," he

says. "They josh her around in the bar till she staggers home. Hey, sister, you're leakin'. You can always find Dot, just follow the dribbles. My ass, says Dotty doing her fingers at them like this. I dunno if I could find it in all them folds, says one. That brown hole, says another. Is that a dead mouse or Dot's twat I smell? You hear some rich things at Tod's. I stop in for a beer when I feel like it. Never talked to those shitheads. One of them asked me for a light. I gave it to him. That's about it. We had a neighborhood meeting, the alderman arranged it after the complaints, but you could see Tod's in tight with him. You can't get anything done in this city. I gave up calling the police."

"Dotty's certainly foul," says Lou thinking about it.

"She fires it right back. You call that a dick, she says. She's in there every night tanking up. They love her."

"I'm glad I live in the back," says Lou. "I still hear it. The bikers rev up in the middle of the night."

"Wait till July. You'll go crazy. Hey, this'll be some climb in these clouds. Look how low—"

15

When they get out of the trees they do not see beyond the slope they are on. They might catch a glimpse through clouds to a patch of meadow in the valley, but it closes up again fast enough. All they see of the world is a hundred yards of this slope. The scrub is sparse. They are to the bare rock.

There is no wind, no more parting of clouds. Of course no

one else is climbing. In silence they take their steps, not as if they are climbing. It does not seem a slope, simply that the world is at that angle. They are not moving toward anything.

Nonetheless it does end. Now their hundred-yard view shows a dome with rounded rock sloping away in every direction. It might be a tiny planetoid they are on, in misty space.

Lou is more out of breath than Lew. They sit down, look, shake out their boots and spread their toes with their fingers.

"A bit on the cold side," says Lew. "Not my idea of having climbed a mountain. I have a better view from my apartment."

Lou wonders if Lew knows his view is of Lou's window and what he has seen.

"Actually, who needs a view? If you see miles it covers the same amount of your eyes. Ever think of that? We could see the city from here, the tall buildings. So what? We see millions of tiny droplets around us instead. What would that little kid call this mist? Suspended pipi of God?"

"I don't think he knows suspended," says Lou.

"Suspended," Lew says, "hanging down from, something like that. That's what makes that German of theirs more like a poem. I read this book about the meaning of words. Take a word like, say, independence. You have your own idea of that word, but you don't see it because it's what they call derived from Latin. I learn a lot from books. See, in German they have their own word, I memorized it, Un-abhängigkeit. Sure sounds like German, doesn't it? Means exactly the same. Un-off-hanging-ness. You can see it, not hanging off something. We don't have that in English. In-de-pen-dence. English borrows everything."

"Interesting," says Lou.

"You should read up on it. No wonder those little boys have a hard time."

"Not to mention spelling," says Lou.

"Hey, fuck spelling. N-i-g-h-t. Beat that! In German you can pronounce the damn words. Like V equals F, see? I figured out how to pronounce all of German just reading a book. Try that on English, sucker."

"You really don't need your ID for the library?" Lou asks, suddenly thinking of it.

"Hey, I got other IDs, but I like to own my books. Once I read it I want it there to refer to. I'm always referring to this and that. I found a slew of paperbacks someone must've dropped off for the rummage sale. They trust people to leave boxes outside the Community Center. You get a lot of things there after dark. Hey, and I'm a master at slipping that shiny new paperback under my coat into my armpit and walking nonchalantly out of a store. Did you know what a scummy character I am?"

"I had an idea," says Lou taking it lightly.

"Well, I'm not so bad. I like to talk it up. One thing I don't resort to is the line that the whole world shits so you ought to cheat and steal. I'm practical. I wouldn't do anything I might get caught at."

"I never stole anything," says Lou.

"Hey, what do you do?" Lew asks. "Of course I talk on and don't ask you anything. I wonder if I'm interested in other people at all. What does it take to be interested in someone else?"

"I signed up with an agency to spend a year in Central America," says Lou.

"I haven't got around to checking out Central America," Lew says.

"It was a place called Mosquitia claimed by Honduras and Nicaragua both. It's not the sort of place you'd like to go. Swampy forest, mosquitoes—"

"Hey, can you see the travel posters? Vacation in Mosquitia! View of a swamp with bugs all over it. Hell, I don't have to leave my backyard in the suburbs for that, buster! Someone blew it naming that country. Nobugsia, that's my country."

"I was supposed to teach English. It wasn't the most useful thing. I spent a lot of time drinking."

"My sort of place."

"The men don't do anything but sit and drink. I read a monograph from the subsubbasement at the library, no one had taken it out since it was written, on the drinking habits of Mosquitians. The author got a grant to go down and drink for a year."

"I'm into it. Hey, that's an idea for a scheme. I need a new one soon. I've been thinking of getting out of here."

Lou wants to keep talking. "I spent a lot of time in a sort of open-air bar, a roof but no walls, down by the water. We drank and talked, not about much. I played the guitar. There was a coatimundi on a rope pacing back and forth on a branch just outside. I read a book about coatimundis recently."

"Anus Dei qui tollis coatimundi," says Lew suddenly inspired, but Lou needs the joke explained. "It's from the Mass. I was raised Catholic. Anus instead of Agnus? Never mind. It's Latin. Why do you read all these things about Mosquitia if you've already been there? I'd be trying to forget a place like that."

"I'm trying to remember it," says Lou.

"You working on some research project? I thought you had a grant."

"Searching and researching," says Lou not entirely lying.

"And re-researching," says Lew. "Don't I know."

"I lost everything I had in my fire. Except my rug because it was at the cleaners that week—"

"What, notes and things, files?"

Lou nods in a way that does not indicate yes but more that he is pondering.

Lew can understand it is not a topic to pursue and must not be particularly interested anyway. "I read books to get ideas for new schemes," he says. "You don't know when the next one will come. I'm an omnivore when it comes to books. There's one of those English words, omnivore! I bet in German it's something you can see. You know what Germans call the West? They call it Evening Land."

"Do you have any idea what Fonta Zee means?" Lou asks having wondered about it for some time. "Something like Blurda Fonta Zee."

"Sounds French," says Lew. "Blur is French for blue, I think."

"It was something Hanno said. Something Hanno said Niko said—"

"Doesn't sound German. Blue of the fantasy. Fantasy out of the blue, maybe. That's Hanno, out of the blue."

"It wouldn't be French," says Lou.

"I'm cold," Lew says rubbing his toes and beginning to put his socks back on. "So the men spend their time drinking? I'm thinking about that six-pack in my car."

"I could use more a hot cup of coffee," says Lou, "in this cold." He shakes out his clammy socks before stretching them over his heels.

"A beer always does the trick," Lew says. "Hey, aren't those kids little buggers? Turns out a friend of mine knows their mother. Hardly speaks English. She came over for the VA benefits."

"I've never seen her," says Lou. "I've heard her."

"Their father got killed in a Jeep crash. He was a lieutenant in the army. It's something when someone dies in your family. My mother died when I was in third grade."

Lou looks at Lew who is tying up his leather bootlaces and does not look sad. Lou does not know if he should sympathize. He would, but Lew is not the sort to want him to.

"That's a long time ago," says Lew. "I would be somebody else now if it hadn't happened. That's a thing you're sure makes you into somebody else. I'm just a placeholder for the Lew I would have been. Hey, where's your family? They alive?"

"They live up around here," Lou says, "farther north."

"I like getting out, coming up here," says Lew. "Even this has been a good afternoon. Just the climbing, that's enough. A little sit, a little talk, wiggle the toes, and down for a few beers."

They come down fast over the boulders. When they get down their legs tingle as if they are already drunk. They lie back on a mossy patch and have a couple of beers each and then open their thirds and warm up in the car. When the defroster has dried the mist from inside the windows, they back out.

They pass the ranger's Jeep where he is sitting eating a sandwich and drinking coffee. Lew blows a friendly honk, and they are on their way back to the city in the beginning of heavy rain. The wipers flop irregularly, a sign of the car's age.

16

It stayed sunny in the city. This was the day Judy had planned to quit her job. She had been afraid she would not do it. On her afternoon coffee break she could go out on the lawn and get some sun instead. She could unwrap her skirt and lie on it in her maillot. All she needs to go to work these warm days is a maillot, her wraparound and flip-flop sandals.

Judy keeps all her clothes in one box. Her maillots are stretchy nylon and fold up tiny. She has a few denim wraparounds. In winter she wears tights under them and nylon turtlenecks, and her down jacket squeezes into a little pouch the way her sleeping bag does. The only large things are her balloony white rubber winter boots insulated by air pockets. She likes to go through the list of her possessions and think how lightweight everything is.

When Lou and Lew were reaching the mountain's top, Judy was holding her Styrofoam coffee cup looking out the glass door, the only way to see what the weather was. People were walking by without jackets on. She wondered why the man she thinks of as Lew had not come in yet.

She likes Lew, but he is unattractive. She thought of attractive Pete, even though she does not always like him. Why not Lew? He has unwashed brown hair she would not like to touch. He wears baggy clothes and sometimes has not noticed his fly is unzipped or his shoelace is untied. He has a pocky sort of complexion and dirty semicircles under his fingernails. If she could take off his clothes and scrub him down and put him into something clean and bright, stretched tightly over him without wrinkles, like Pete wears, and comb that hair and get at where he missed shaving— She decided he would still not be attractive. It is the way he slumps.

Judy turned away from the door and knew she must quit today, could not still put it off. She left her empty cup on her desk and went looking for Mr. Wagstaff. He was not in his office behind her desk. He was not by the coffee machine on the mezzanine. Someone told her he was supervising the rearrangement of noncirculating periodicals in the subsubbasement. Judy headed down the concrete stairs holding the fat metal tube of a banister. Her sandals flopped against the concrete. In the basement she went to the little door and used her key.

It was quiet on the subbasement level, the stacks of shelves disappearing in darkness. She went down the last flight. It was also quiet there. At the end of one aisle a light came from one of the stacks. Her sandals flopped on the wettish floor. A dehumidifier hummed. Judy heard sudden clumsy noises. As she got there the fat boy who retrieves books was getting up from kneeling in front of tall thin Mr. Wagstaff and pushed a row of bound periodicals off a shelf with his butt. Mr. Wagstaff was red-faced to see Judy.

"Mr. Wagstaff," she said.

He told the boy to go on rearranging and walked down the aisle with Judy. "Things get ahead of me," he said. "The months go by and volumes keep coming and coming from the bindery, and there I am cramming them in. I'm shoving everything over two stacks and monographs up to the Annex Attic. So what lures you to these depths? Tub's the only one to go down here, I thought. Haven't come here myself for months. Didn't I have you reading these shelves when you first came? We're due for another job soon. Can't have Tub do it. I'm surprised he finds anything without ballocksing us all up."

"Mr. Wagstaff," said Judy, "I would've come to see you on my morning break, but I couldn't find you."

"I've been down here working this out, measuring. The Annex Attic has enough space since that stuff went to the Special Collections Wing. So much to juggle."

"I'm going to have to be giving you a month's notice on my job, Mr. Wagstaff, I'm sorry," Judy said.

"Oh that's a shame," he said stopping still. "You're good to have at Circulation." They were beside the loud-humming dehumidifier.

Judy said, "It's that I'll be moving away, because the person I live with is moving."

"Oh that's a shame," said Mr. Wagstaff. "So you have to go. I can't entice you to stay. I suppose I can move Jean down from Acquisitions. Jean's been wanting to try Circulation, doesn't like lonely office work. How's it coming, Tub?"

Tub puffed from the lighted stack.

"I would have told you earlier," Judy said, "but Pete didn't know till now."

"It won't be a problem," Mr. Wagstaff said. "I'm used to the turnover. Pete? Oh yes, Pete."

"I better get back to the desk," Judy said.

"We'll miss you," Mr. Wagstaff said. "We'll have a little party for you. When will you be going?"

Judy told the story she had spent the morning making up about what she and Pete would do, go west where Pete would repair pianos and she would make kites to sell. She has an artistic side, she told Mr. Wagstaff.

When the mountain climbers were putting their boots on

again, Judy was on her way up the concrete stairs, realizing then that when she came down to the subsubbasement she almost caught Mr. Wagstaff in the act, as she imagined it, with Tub.

17

Lew drops Lou off. He has some other place to go.

"What dwive you in dat caw? I not dwive in caws," says Hanno when Lou walks up to the door and sits on the stoop. His legs are stiffening from the climb. "How can it be two Lous?" asks Hanno.

"We spell it different," says Lou.

"Oh God not again. Apropos I tell you somefing Miss O'Weilly say in English aw fwee ways you spell two. Miss O'Weilly aw you cwazy? I have always wookbook wook-book wookbook. I neva finish."

"Hanno, why are you wearing those rubber gloves? Gonna wash dishes?"

"What aw you cwazy? I find dat not funny." He folds his hands in front of his stomach and looks at his fingers twin-ing. "I find dese wubba gloves vewy à la mode." He keeps watching his fingers twine, then he says, "In Frankfurtz we say Handschuh dat mean shoe faw de hand dummy. De mama give dis note I show Miss O'Weilly."

Hanno pulls a crinkled slip of paper from his left pocket. He carefully unfolds it and holds it for Lou to see. It says, "Excuse gloves four his eczemas, Mrs. Leroy Alphonse."

Lou feels as if a tear is coming into his eye and Hanno

might see it. Hanno scrunches the note back into his pocket. "The gloves are neat," Lou says, "like a spaceman's."

"What spaceman? Niko all de time watch Sixty-six Sixty-six Sixty-six what we say Stawship Entapwise. In Frankfurtz have we also Entapwise. Wight now Niko watch it dat can I tell you. Miss O'Weilly she tell me de staws and de planates."

Across the street Dotty has come out still in her slip. She looks over at Hanno and Lou without smiling.

"I find dat lady not fwendly," says Hanno. "Mama talk to her she say goddamn you to Mama."

"She's growing tomatoes there," says Lou. "Someday you'll see her big red tomatoes."

A window on the second floor pulls up. Niko yells down, "Hanno it is ova de Entapwise. Mama say come."

Hanno keeps the tomatoes in his mind because the next morning he tells Lou a dream.

Lou is coming down the stairs with a load of due books. First Niko comes busting out his door. "Well am late," he yells at Lou. "Miss Forp get mad I wun all de way." He leaps down the stairs missing half of them. He is out the front door when Hanno comes out and Lou gets to that landing.

"Morning, Hanno," says Lou.

"Special stawt afta uvva alweady stawt," Hanno says wearing his gloves. He walks down the stairs beside Lou not saying anything.

"You quiet today," says Lou. "Last night you talked a blue streak."

"What is dat blue stweak?" he says in a deadish voice. "I have only no Lust to talk get de point."

"What is Loost?" Lou asks.

"Dat can you not in English say. We say Lust. Dat weally

when you want somefing. Dat is vewy good to have Lust. Lustig dat when you happy auf deutsch. I teach you."

When they go out the front Hanno suddenly looks worried. "I not cwoss de stweet," he says. "De lady wif de tomato—"

"She won't bother you," says Lou, but he walks on the street side so Hanno can hide beside him. His school is in the direction of the library for a few blocks.

"I have de scawiest dweam. I wake up scweam to Mama."

"What about?" asks Lou.

"I can it you not say," says Hanno.

"You can tell me," says Lou. "I have bad dreams."

"I get in de mama's bed. She put de lights on all de lights. De dweam go away."

"What was it?"

Hanno says nothing as they walk. They come to a street and wait for cars. They walk down the next block not saying anything. Lou's legs are stiff. Hanno has his workbook under his arm, and he flips at the edges of the pages with his fingers in the pink rubber gloves. At the next crossing Hanno has to go to the left.

"It was a giant tomato so big as de building," he says spreading his arms wide, workbook in one hand. "So big I tell you. You know what can de tomatoes when you put in de fawk in de tomato you know what de tomatoes can do how dey explode all de wed explode all ova? You know dat?" He looks at Lou's cocked head to see if he understands. "In de dweam I can tell you de giant tomato it would explode all ova all de wed and dose what you call dose howwible fings?"

"Seeds?"

"Dose howwible seeds and de wed what we say Schleim—"

"Slime?"

"It come out de skin. De giant tomato it would soon explode I know dat."

"Did it in the dream?"

"It would explode I tell you dat. It would. I wun to Mama scweaming scweaming. She put on all de lights."

18

It is Niko he sees when he comes home from a day beside the canal. Lou is getting browner, good for his bad complexion. He had taken his shirt off and rolled his pant legs up to his knees.

"In free weeks is my birfday," says Niko dancing a bit on his heels. "I ask Mama faw dwums well I mean drrums."

"Drums?"

"You know drums," Niko says making his hands pound in the air and a wild face. "What I want to have. In de school I pwactice in Music Skills Pewiod." Niko is excited telling Lou this, forgets his R's. He does his wild drumming again in the air and starts spinning and dancing off around the corner of the building. Lou remembers his own quiet instrument that was burned.

Up in his room he stares at the five telephone wires. He thinks what sound they would make if he could strum them. A guitar with strings that long and far apart, a chord so deep it would hang there making slow waves in the air— A huge guitar outside his window lying on its side between his room and Lew's, an invisible wind guitar— With his open window Lou imagines that deep humming sound. It is trucks though, far off.

In the morning he goes to the Consignment and Resale Shop two blocks up the street. They have had guitars when he has walked by. The man tells him to come back late tomorrow. He does and there is a guitar, not a good one but cheap.

He carries it into his room when the sun is edging up the back wall, the rug shadowy again. Because he is sticky he takes off everything. His pale section from below his belly button to his knees, a person of two colors— He would like to go without clothes, which never fit him. In Mosquitia he would wear the same white pants and shirt as everyone else.

Now comes the music of his lonesome evening. To the deep hum of the wind guitar he adds first the sounds of tuning his strings. They get as close to right as they will. Radio sounds float in the window if the wind blows that way, a song he recognizes that interferes with his own rhythms, or a Latin number from what might be Lew's FM.

Across the alley he sees how high the morning glory vines have grown up to the crosspiece of the window, but no flowers yet. He could not see Lew's guitar on the shelf if the lights were on, only the very top shelves of Lew's books. On the sill he can vaguely see the shape of the cat crouched behind the leaves as if a forest animal. Bird songs do come up from the ailanthus tree, not songs but squeep-squeeps of city birds. The cat is interested.

To these Lou adds the slow harp notes of his guitar. It is not a song that comes to him but strumming such as he would do late afternoons in the corner of the open-air bar, gentle unnoticed music behind the men's talking. Once he finds himself coinciding with a radio, but his voice is not worth his listening to.

The sun edges up the wall. Now a dog yaps. He has not heard the rooftop door flapping for some days. Has she asked them to fix it? At the library he said he would take Judy to the beach on Sunday in his car depending on the weather.

The Fourth Reich is arriving. The cycles blast by, screech and settle. Lou plays his guitar on his naked lap. If he was in Mosquitia, if there was a low murmur of men in white at sunset and the lap of slow waves of the lagoon— Kikatu would still be on his branch, alive, pacing. A snarl might come from him. Where would the Mosquitian women be? All at home.

A siren in the distance, but not to come get the Fourth Reich, too much to hope— The siren goes its own way somewhere else. Dark enough now for the little boys to be in bed. Niko will sleep, but Hanno and his dream? Lou strums his slow notes as if Hanno could hear them. He watches his own fingers over the strings.

Now the noises from the room below begin for the night so loud Lou can hear though he plays, a swooping moan that goes from the sound of a woman to the sound of a man, someone jumping and landing on the floor, spinning, dancing.

A bottle smashes down on the sidewalk, and from that direction a fight begins. Lou holds his silent guitar, no thoughts—

19

The wind is so steady the bumblebee kite stays up in one high spot and Judy can lie on her back holding the string. She lies on her wraparound, Lou lies on the sand with his pant legs rolled up and his wadded-up shirt to rest his head on. The yellow and black bumblebee flies above them. The string connects it to Judy, but the sky is too bright to see the whole string. It disappears, and there alone far above it is the steady bumblebee.

"I'd like an inflatable raft," says Judy. "I'd lie on my back on the waves flying my kite. I feel too plunked down on this sand."

"I like it," says Lou, "the waves lapping it."

"My friend has a raft," she says. "I should've borrowed it. It's a good thing you have a car. We can come here lots. He has the use of a car, he says, for his job, but he can't use it after hours. Who can go to the beach on a weekday? He doesn't even come take me out for a drive on my lunch hour. I've never seen this so-called car he has the use of. He's such a shithead, I can't trust a thing he says."

"You still like him?"

"If you met him— Well, you wouldn't like him. He's the opposite of you. Pete's his name."

From the raft Lou thought for a moment Judy's friend could possibly be Lew, but if he cannot use his car after hours and Lou used Lew's car to get to the beach, Lou decides Judy's Pete cannot be Lew by another name.

"I got my car at the government auction," Lou says. "That's why it says Interagency Motor Pool on the doors."

"That's the kind Pete has the use of," says Judy. "He drives government cars. His must be the newer model though. Maybe they bought his when they sold off yours. You can get a lot of things from government surplus, Pete's raft, my insulated air boots. They develop great things for the army. I'm waiting for space surplus, then I'll be in heaven. You weren't in the army? Pete evaded the draft."

"I had a safe number back then," says Lou.

"When I was in Mort's yesterday— How come I never bump into you there since that once? Don't you eat? Boy do I eat! I have a fast metabolism. Anyway, I was in Mort's and I bumped into that German woman again, you know her? She's a wreck. She doesn't know anyone to talk to. She was trying to ask me where she could buy a drum. I have no idea. Not in Mort's. We were talking. What I'm getting at is the army. She tried to explain again about her husband, this black lieutenant in the army. I asked her why she married an American. She held me by the wrist and told me this story about when she was a little girl and the war was still on. She remembers it. She lived on a farm in some mountains I don't know where. She said, I can't do her accent, how she stood in her mama's garden and watched the light of Cologne burning behind the mountains. Her father was fighting in the east. She didn't say if he was a Nazi. And then later when they knew we were coming, the Americans, only they weren't sure, it might be the Russians, they were hoping for Americans, less likelihood of being raped, her mama and her aunt she lived with— They're hiding down in the basement of their farmhouse hearing the troops roll by. They hear noises, stomping around, and the door at the top of the stairs swings open and in the light is a big American with a grenade, a black man, it turns out. He sees it's a little girl and her mama and aunt, and he laughs, puts his grenade back, or whatever you do, and comes down the stairs and gives the little girl a chocolate bar and picks her up. She never saw a black man in Germany in the war. He pick me up in arms, that's how she said it. Her mama and aunt were just crying, being happy. She wanted to tell me her life story, I got the feeling. She hasn't talked to anyone since she got here except the VA and me. I can't understand her English. I probably got the story wrong. The American soldier set her free was the idea. So she grew up with a thing for black men, I suppose. Her father died on the Russian front. And her mother's dead, and her aunt— She's having a hard time over here. She had a hard time finding this place, raising the kids. She was talking on and on, and I finally had to get out of there, it was too much. Hope you find a drum, I said."

The wind has dropped while they have forgotten to be looking at the kite. "It's dipping," says Lou.

"It's going in the water!" Judy yells, leaping up and running fast down the sand. Lou gets up and runs along but does not catch up. The bumblebee is falling faster than Judy runs. It hits a wave, and Judy stomps up and down on the sand. When Lou catches up, she does not really seem mad. "I suppose I've had enough for today," she says, wrapping the string round and round and watching the soggy bee slip over the waves toward shore and wash up on the sand. "This one's done for," she says. "It didn't cost much."

Back in the parking lot Judy sees the shed marked MEN at one end and WOMEN at the other. "Excuse me, I have to go to the loo," she says and disappears.

Lou opens the car windows and lets out the hot air. When Judy comes back she says, "Nothing personal. Should've said go to the john. In my family we always called it the loo."

20

Lou walks up the stairs to his door. He uses his new key because of the guitar and all the library books. The air is stuffy. He leaves the door open a bit and opens the window. He lies down and might be falling asleep.

He is aware of a cat. He leans his head back and looks upside down at a cat padding in the door with a thing in its teeth. The cat moves along the wall, and Lou bends his neck watching it. It comes around to his feet. That is a gray mouse in its teeth. It drops it, sits and stares at it.

Lou sits up. The mouse looks dead on its back. The cat taps at it once with its paw, sits back and watches again. The mouse quickly flips over and tries to run. "Get it," says Lou. The cat catches the mouse in its teeth. Lou should get it and step on it out of mercy.

The cat paces around the room with the gray limp mouse's tail dangling. When the cat leaps onto the sill and settles, Lou recognizes it as Lew's, the familiar way it flaps its tail. Lou sits watching it slowly do in the mouse. The dead mouse is not as much fun. The cat has heard those bird squeeps in the tree below from a new angle. The tree is closer under Lou's window than under Lew's.

Lew's window is green with leaves now, Lou cannot even see the top of the bookshelf. Lou himself has almost enough borrowed books to fill his own shelves, he has his own guitar, no bed but a rug, his own green curtain dangling unhooked, and now the very cat on the sill. Who let it in downstairs?

He reaches in his pocket and finds the crinkled pink slip

from that time when he had begun to write L-o-u. He smooths it out, then crinkles it again, expecting the cat to look over, ready to chase, but the slip is sweaty from the pocket and does not make the right sound. Even when he flips it across the floor, this cat is not interested.

He thinks of his own cat he had until the fire. He thinks of his old guitar he had carried over his head in the flood, his old shelves and books, the ones he stored in his family's barn when he went to Mosquitia then brought to the city to his new place, which did not last long. What were those books about?

The fire began in the wires at night. Perhaps a mouse had chewed through something between the floors. No one heard anything. The people below were asleep. It was their ceiling light that caught on fire. Lou was in a heavy sleep from too much to drink.

His cat started tearing around, making yowls. He tried to shut it up, cuffed it once, then he smelled burning. He stood up in a daze. The floorboards were very hot on his feet. The people downstairs were screaming. Was he awake? He did not move for a moment.

Then his floor was on fire. The yellow came through between the boards and lapped around to meet itself. From the center of the room, where the ceiling light downstairs was, it spread. His guitar was on the floor. It went like kindling. Lou was jumping into his pants and looking for the cat. Flames began to edge up the walls, were touching the first shelf of books. Under the window they had caught the sheet hanging off the end of his bed. There was the cat on the sill, the fire between Lou and it. He could not do anything. He had to get out. Out, down the stairs, the people below screaming down the stairs too, onto the street—

He watched, shivering in only his pants, with the people on the sidewalk looking up. Sirens came from everywhere. Someone had seen the cat fly out the window. Lou went over to that side, but the firemen had blocked it off. He thought he saw his limp dead cat on the cement.

It was fall weather. Someone gave him a sweater, and he found old rubber boots in the trash can where he left his dead cat in a bag in the morning. He had the slip for the cleaners in those pants pockets, so he picked up his clean saved rug, and he forgot everything else. He thumbed his way to the mountains, where he could stay with his family for the cold winter. He got through it all right.

21

He is sitting on the stoop with Lew late in the evening. Eight motorcycles are lined up shining outside Tod's. Their gas tanks are red with a big white dot and on it the black swastika.

"They can do that in public?" Lou asks.

Lew sips his beer. "It's what they do in private— Hey, talk about in private—" He takes a long sip then looks at Lou as his grin spreads. "It's what I saw last night. I'm almost ashamed I kept watching, but I'd look at anything, I admit it. One of my windows, it looks out at the brick wall of your building, not much of a view— That's why I grow morning glories outside that window. Last night I was in bed, in the dark, alone for once, ha-ha. Well, I can't get to sleep so I sit up and put my chin on the sill and look at the darkness through the leaves. There's a light on the second floor, and I think, oh, maybe that's Lou's—"

"No," says Lou.

"Well, I realize now, but I'm looking. I can see it between the branches of that tree. I'm looking right down onto a king-size white sheet on a bed. Always before that window had a shade down. Not last night, boy. There's a shadow passing across the sheet, and I keep looking, I admit it. Then this naked guy leaps from somewhere down onto the bed, waving his crank around and going to town. A tall thin guy, hairy and wild, and he starts slapping his own ass. I barely hear these wild moans he's making. Then he's on his knees pouncing around the bed, slapping away and grunting, it sounds like, a deep grunting I thought I could hear. Then he reaches down over the edge and brings up, I couldn't see what, but a little bottle he unscrews, I guess, his drug, and takes a hit off it up his nose. He starts turning red, and whoo! he's off again cranking away. Beat that!"

"I did hear something last night half asleep," says Lou.

"You can say one thing, he's a master, I don't know what of. Whoo! his big old crank starts to explode, and he flops down rolling on the bed, spouting. He lies there for a while. I'm still looking. Then he rolls off, and all I see is a shadow moving across the sheet. Then there he is, dressed in a suit and tie, his hair slicked down, he doesn't look wild, and he's kneeling on the bed, reaches up and pulls the shade. In a second the light behind goes off. That's all, tune in tomorrow."

"He's there alone?" asks Lou. "I never seen anyone go in that door." Lou fiddles with the flip top of his can. "Speaking of—"

Lew looks up from his beer and tosses the can into the gutter.

"Was that your cat that sauntered in my door yesterday? It sauntered out again in a while taking its dead mouse with it."

"Could have been. She goes down the fire escape and checks things out. She's on her own."

"Maybe Hanno or Niko let her in downstairs," Lou says finishing his last drop.

22

In these weeks of taking out ten books a day Lou has his shelves full because each ten lasts three weeks. Now he is taking out biographies of dictators of Honduras and Nicaragua. It depends on the book, one says this man was a hero, another says he was a thug. Lou plans to get to periodicals soon, even if they are noncirculating and he has to read them there. He can take other books home to keep his shelves full. But he must see what has happened recently. Nicaragua may have withdrawn its claim.

He comes up the steps of the library with his due books under his arm. Judy told him this would be her last day. He goes through the glass door.

Judy has swiveled in her chair. He sees the back of her head as she combs her short hair. She has a string of white pop-pearls around her neck and earrings of little white seashells. The white shoulder straps of her maillot, not the one she wore to the beach, make her skin look darker than it did in red.

She reaches under her chair and gets something from her purse, a tiny bottle of cologne. She unscrews it and dabs behind each ear. Lou is about to put his books on the desk where it says RETURN BOOKS HERE. A man in a suit and tie comes out of his office with his eyes twinkling.

"May I have the honor, Miss Spree?" he says rubbing his hands. "Tub'll watch the desk. Don't you look nice!"

"All set," Judy says in good spirits but keeping her voice down in the library. When she comes from behind the desk she sees Lou. "Lew!" she whispers as loudly as she can and bounces up to give him a kiss on his cheek. "We're celebrating. Come to my party. You're my faithfulest customer."

"Lew?" says the man in his speaking voice. He slips back into his office and is out again in a moment. "Is this you?" he says, whispering. He hands Lou an overdue notice on a postcard addressed to Lewis Tennant at Lew's address.

"I don't have any books overdue," whispers Lou.

The man hands him another postcard. "Is this you?" And he hands him another. "And is this you?"

Each card is stamped RETURN TO SENDER—ADDRESSEE UNKNOWN. "I know I returned—" Lou begins.

"Three notices— That book is not in the stacks." The man has turned red.

"He always returns books, Mr. Wagstaff," Judy whispers. "Maybe Tub blew it again, forgot to take out the slip, stuck it in the wrong place."

"Can I see your ID, Mr. Tennant?" Mr. Wagstaff says in a low voice.

Lou pulls out Lew's ID and hands it to him.

"I'm going to put an Invalid sticker on this until you locate that book, sir." He slips back into his office.

Lou looks at the three overdue notices, addressee unknown. It is the book about coatimundis. He returned it weeks ago, the day he met the little boys, he is sure. The notice gives the borrowing rules in small print.

204 • COMPANION PIECES

"I'll straighten it out this afternoon," Judy says under her breath. "It was definitely Tub."

Mr. Wagstaff comes back with the invalid card. "As you know, you'll have to return any other books you've borrowed," he whispers. "That's the rule after three notices. It's how I run the library." He punches what must be Lew's number into the machine behind the desk. It starts printing out the names of all Lou's books. "My God," says Mr. Wagstaff out loud, "where does this end!" The machine keeps printing.

Judy looks at Lou standing there slumped.

"You'll need a truck!" says Mr. Wagstaff.

"You don't feel like the party, Lew?" Judy says quietly.

"I'll go back to my room," he says.

"Tub!" calls Mr. Wagstaff, and the only other person in the reading room looks up annoyed from her corner. "Judy, I'll be wanting you to show Jean the ropes after lunch." They head up the stairs to the mezzanine. Judy waves good-bye down to Lou.

As he heads for the glass door with his printout and the invalid card, he sees a fat boy squeeze in behind Judy's desk and sit there with his mouth hanging open, all set for the next borrower.

23

Lou carries books back all evening. He slips them in the off-hours book return slot. He wants them out of his room, off his shelves. He cannot sleep till they are gone.

He sleeps late in the morning behind his green curtain, spends the afternoon playing his guitar and sipping from a bottle he supplied himself with last night.

When the sun is low he hears drumming and remembers Niko's birthday. A few days ago he bought a plastic car at the Community Center rummage sale. He goes down the stairs with it. Niko is marching down from the second landing, a toy drum hanging from his neck. Brap brap brrrr brap brap brrrr— He stomps out the door. Lou follows.

On the stoop Niko pounds as loud as he can. Brap! Brap! Brap! Brap! He rolls the sticks: Brrrrrrrr!

Lew is getting out of his car. He always parks right in front of Lou's building. As Lou comes out the door, Lew is saying, "Kid, that drum's just what my hangover doesn't need."

Brap! Brap! Brap! Brap!

"Is that your birthday present?" Lou asks.

"Mama have give me dis drum. I am seven."

"Congratulations," says Lew.

Brap! Brap!

"Could you tone it down?" Lew asks holding his forehead.

"Mama say go outside wif drum. I say it right with drum." He holds the sticks about to pound then looks at Lew under his curly hair. "Have you birfday present for me?"

Lew shows his empty hands.

Lou says, "Here, Niko, I got you something."

Niko drops the sticks and grabs the brown bag in Lou's hands. He pulls out the green plastic car. "I like it," he says. "Fank you well I mean ththank you."

He takes the drum from his neck and puts it on the stoop beside the sticks and looks at the car.

"I'll show you," says Lou. He revs it up rolling the wheels

fast on his hand then sets it on the sidewalk and off it goes by itself till it runs down.

"Here come Kool-Aid!" yells Niko.

The car keeps him busy. Lou and Lew sit on the stoop watching him. "I could stand a little kid like that," says Lew.

Lou holds the drum on his lap. Niko drives the car back up to the stoop.

"Mama have me not give de real drum what I wanted," he says, "what is on Sixty-six. Peter Platypus play on cartoons. You know." He makes his hands pound in the air and a wild face. "What you call wif cymbals? What I pwac-practice in Music Skills Period." He goes off pounding the air, dancing and singing around the corner of the building.

"He'll be back," says Lou.

When Niko comes back he sits down and explains. "Mama not good understand. She cannot English. I love Mama when also she not get me drum like Peter Platypus with cymbals. You know it cost money."

"I had a guitar someone left behind," says Lew. "I didn't want it. I sold it to the consignment man up the street."

Niko asks Lou to hold his car while he puts on the drum again and starts marching around, back and forth. Brap! Brap! Brap! Lew holds his forehead.

Hanno comes out on the stoop and rolls his eyes. He sits down between Lew and Lou.

"Hey, dishwasher from outer space! Whatcha got there?" asks Lew.

Brap brrrr brrrr—

Hanno is holding a half-eaten chocolate bar with his rubber gloves. "We have pawty faw my bwuvva dat cwazy one. De mama give me dis special while it not my buffday. See you dis Schokolade?"

"Shocko Lodda?" wonders Lou.

Brap! Brap!

"Dis come fwom acwoss de sea. Dis come fwom what we say my Heimat. How say you dat?"

"Homeland," says Lew. "Vaterland."

"Dis come fwom my Heimat. See you dis witing? Dat is deutsch. Dat can I wead. Scho-ko-la-de see you?"

Brrrrrrrr!

"Oh," says Lou. "Shocko Lodda!"

24

That printout on its striped green-and-white paper folded back and forth lies on a shelf where the books were. All his shelves are empty. The guitar, which may have been Lew's, lies on the rug beside Lou who stretches his arm out and plucks a string when it is getting dark. He plucks it again very hard and a third time so hard the string breaks. He stops himself before smashing his fist on the guitar.

He has finished another bottle, another day of sitting there as the sun passes and drinking. He is trying to remember Mosquitia. He does not know quite enough to remember it now. What has he lost? He cannot see Kikatu's face in his head, the expression he made when he snarled. These coatis woven into his rug are not Kikatu.

And the pelicans, he thinks, are not diving into the lagoon. He cannot see their speed, they are not upside down. And these little boys— Lou has felt this way before.

He gave Niko that little car for his birthday. How old will Hanno be? Nine?

Blat! Blat! go the motorcycles revving up to leave the bar. When they are gone and it is quiet—

The weather is cooling a bit.

No bluish light from behind the morning glory leaves—

Smash goes a bottle on the street. And mumbly laughter— It is not the man downstairs.

He remembers that Honduras means "the Depths." Nicaragua means "Black Water." There are whole families of dictators down there.

"I'm gonna fuckin' smash your ass!"

"You fuckin'—" It goes on.

Kaka pipi, thinks Lou. He would almost laugh lying on his rug in the dark.

Melons bobbing up around him and floating alongside—

Blat! One cycle takes off around the block, but it is back soon enough. Lew said he has given up calling the police.

Blat Blat Blat Blat Blat—

I would go down and shoot them, thinks Lou, like a wild gunman.

I would set their tanks on fire.

I would go down and tell them to shut the fuck up.

This is not what Lou would do, but after all the nights of—

He stands up, pulls his pants on, rolls down his cuffs. He unwads the shirt he uses for a pillow, pulls it over his head. He pulls his boots over his bare heels and does not tie the laces, forgets to zip his fly. He opens the door. Dim light from the light bulb on the second landing— These creaky stairs—

The motorcycles are muffled on the windowless stairs.

No light in the crack under the door of Mrs. Alphonse's apartment, no light under the other door, the back one. The light over the stoop has burned out.

Lou stands on the stoop.

Two men slam each other against the brick wall of Tod's. They are yelling, but the cycles make more noise.

Lou begins to yell louder than he thinks he can. Who can hear him? "Get the fuck out of my neighborhood you goddamn Nazi fuckers you shithead fuckass motorcycles shut the fuck up who can sleep with you fucking assholes—"

Dotty is there in her bathrobe behind her fence.

Good, thinks Lou, an ally. "Who the fuck can sleep you goddamn shithead—" The fight has stopped, the bikers look at him from across the street. He looks at Dotty.

"I'm sick and tired of your language," she yells, but at Lou. "That's one thing I don't have to listen to. If you don't like living next to a bar you can move. What right have you to come out here yelling? You don't catch me yelling in the middle of the night. I've lived here for years. Who do you think you are? I'll call the police on you."

"You bother this lady?" a biker says in a deep voice over to Lou.

"And your colored friends with their drums driving me crazy all day," Dotty yells.

"I can't sleep with this goddamn noise—" Lou says, not as loud.

"Blow it out your asshole," says the biker.

Lou looks over at Dotty, but she is just going inside.

"You better get inside, brother," says a second biker, putting his arm around the first. "Do what the old twat says. That's Dot, she's our pal. She lives here. Don't fuck around. Get inside."

When Lou gets inside he touches his heart with his hand against his chest. They would have killed him on the sidewalk. He is not afraid.

There are no lights under the doors. No one is awake. No one heard him. But why should he go to sleep?

25

Hanno is back early from school. "Miss O'Weilly have meeting faw special we go home," he says to Lou.

Lou is sitting on the stoop after sitting on his rug all morning and past noon. He has nothing to do.

Hanno sits beside him in good spirits and cuts a loud fart. "What! What! Who do dat?" he says not able to stop his smirk.

"Revolting," says Lou.

"What is dat wevolting?" Hanno says. "Dat I find not funny."

The chocolaty fart hits Lou's nose, but he does not move. It blows on the wind down the block.

"Dat is what we say a Furz."

"Foortz?"

"Fawt you dummy. I pwactice pwactice all de time fawting fawting. My bwuvva cannot sleep when I make all de time fawts. I give you anuvva one," Hanno says. It is not quite as loud.

"Miss O'Reilly like your farts?"

"No no I squeeze togevva fawts go back in. Miss O'Weilly not find fawts lovely."

"You ever put shit on her desk?" Lou asks in a bad mood.

"Aw you cwazy what you say de shits on desk?"

Hanno looks at Lou and sees something, the way Lou looks at the sidewalk, the street. Hanno is uncomfortable. He taps his sneaker on the cement.

Lou stares across at the brick wall of Tod's. Hanno looks there too. His eyes bug out when he sees the neon sign in the window. "What! What!" he says.

"What?" says Lou.

"See you dat witing? Miss O'Weilly say sound it out. Ssppii—"

"Spee? Spirits. Fine Spirits and Liquors."

"Ssppiiwwiittss Spiwits am I cwazy dat say Spiwits."

"It doesn't mean what you mean. It's a kind of drink."

"What dwink am I going cwazy wif dis English? De Spiwit dat what I know what it mean Spiwit dis pawt of me always always wif me I tell you."

"It doesn't mean that on the sign," says Lou.

"You fink Spiwit not weal das ist blöde Phantasie. I tell you stupid kaka how you know it is no Spiwit you neva see Spiwit how you say dat?"

"You can believe in your Spirit, Hanno," Lou says.

"Ach du bist so blöd!" Hanno yells squeezing his fists tight in his pink rubber gloves.

"What's blurd?" asks Lou.

"Blöd! Blöd! Dat when you stupid dummy kaka pipi blöd blöd get de point!"

"Calm down," Lou says.

"Why say you always calm down!" yells Hanno. "I make fawts in you face. I put de shits what we say kaka all ova you all ova."

Lou rolls his eyes and leans back against the glass door.

Hanno squeezes his fists and makes noises with the rubber soles of his smudgy sneakers on the sidewalk. He is calming down.

When they have been sitting for a while Hanno says, "Apropos I tell you somefing. You know what is de wings of Satoorn?"

"Saturn? The planet?"

"We say Planate Satoorn why you say Planet we say Planate how funny. You know what is de wings? Dat have Miss O'Weilly say. I tell you dey is a moon dat explode millions millions little pieces of dat moon go wound and wound in de sky."

"Suspended," Lou says.

"What is dat suspended? I tell you de millions pieces de wings of Satoorn. Dey named afta God de planates dat in de systame is. You know what is systame? Dey fit togevva de millions pieces I fink you say gwavity. God make it exact so. Miss O'Weilly say Satoorn he God of de Time he cawwy a sickle what I not know what is dat. She say Hanno dey call him de Gwim Weapa. I find dat not funny. She fat Miss O'Weilly so big boozens. Satoorn de only planate wif wings. But I tell you is weally only one God just one. All fings in de sky named afta God. What de biggest fing in de sky? You know dat you can it now see when you look."

Lou sees a cloud about to pass between them and the sun.

"De sun dat is de biggest I fink it is named most afta God."

"God the Father," says Lou scowling, "and God the Son, all this about God, systems, spirits—"

Hanno looks at Lou's unfriendly face with the pocky complexion. Lou's eyes do not look exactly at Hanno but to one side at nothing. Hanno rubs his gloves together. "What you say de papa de sun aw you cwazy? My papa dead he in awmy jeep tip ova," he says. "You eva see my papa?"

"No."

"I wememba me my papa. Now can I him see wif a hat and de shiny button. He pick me up in awms when I small. Know you how dat is you gwow and gwow so like a balloon when you stawt you little little fing wight inside Mama how is dat? Apropos know you what in de night I can listen to de sounds?"

"Farts," says Lou.

"Not de fawts not de fawts. No no afta de fawts and de bwuvva sleep I fink I am awake. Sometime de uvva side de wall you know what it is I listen what you say de howls. Middle of night de howwible sounds I fink you say howls somefing explode I know dat. I tell you somefing. De Spiwits dey howl in de night. Dat have Miss O'Weilly say. Yes Hanno dat what dey say de Spiwits dey howl in de night and dey fly."

Hanno's hands in his lap, his little feet on the sidewalk— Lou wants to go to his room, hook up his curtain, fall asleep, sleep till morning.

26

When Lou unhooks the curtain there are morning glories all over Lew's window. They have come out this morning, a blue light shining across the alley at him. Lew cannot see them from inside. They are more for Lou to look at. There is no glimpse now of a cat, or a shadow, or knees. Those leaves and morning glories—

Lou sits down and holds his guitar on his lap. He slept in his shirt and pants because it is colder. Lou plays a chord on five strings. He looks at the telephone wires across the sky slightly quiver with the echo of his chord. In that sunlight he could hang by his fingers in a dream.

On his green rug he does not remember Mosquitia. He will have to find Lew, tell him what has happened at the library.

He goes out and around the corner of Lew's building and finds just the number on the button. In a bit Lew comes down the stairs zipping his fly.

"Oh," he says, "caught me in the act. Well, it's early in the morning, ha-ha."

"I invalidated your ID," Lou says handing him the plastic card. "I didn't tell you before."

"Hey, I kept getting these notices. Fuck them. I sent them back. Then yesterday I get this bill for a book about coatimundis!"

"I returned it," says Lou.

"Hey, it's all right. There's no one named Lewis Tennant at this address. They can't find us. But too bad you can't use the library now."

"Well, thanks for the card."

"Good while it lasted, right?" says Lew. "Hey, I've got someone waiting upstairs so I'll see you. We can go for a beer sometime? Did you hear that fight the other night out here? Someone sounded like they were getting killed. I've given up calling the police."

Lou hears him leaping up the stairs. He goes back to his own room. All day he sits and does not play the guitar. The sky clouds up bit by bit. The morning glories turn purple and shrivel. Down the street he hears that door start flapping again.

27

He does have to go out for food. In Mort's Market he sees Judy at the open freezer chest. In just her black maillot and a wraparound she looks cold leaning over it.

"The weather's fouling up," she says when she sees Lou. "Too good to last."

Lou nods.

"We didn't find that book," Judy says. "I told Tub to keep looking. You'll get off the hook. By the way, Lou, it finally hit me, you're not Lew, you're Lou, right, L-o-u? You had a fake ID? That addressee unknown business? I realize I know someone at that address. And once last week you wrote out a pink slip L-o-u-i-s, and I couldn't figure why you misspelled your own name."

Lou smiles, cocks his head at her.

"So you're Lou. I'll see it that way now. Well, I have to get a couple of TV dinners. No time to cook. I'm going away tomorrow, deflating everything, folding it up, and off I go. Finally got my friend with the so-called use of the car to make some use of it. Getting a place down by the beach for the summer. He's coming too, off and on. Going to sublet his place for now."

She picks two TV dinners, and they go to the eight-items-or-less line. Lou has a box of crackers and a chocolate bar.

"Not hungry?" Judy asks. "I'm always hungry. I don't go for frozen food. My friend Pete lives off it. Pop it in, eat it, and off he goes. Once I had the unfortunate experience of unthawing this interesting-looking package in his freezer, figured I'd make something for dinner. You know what it was? Most revolting thing I ever saw—"

Lou knows what it was. "A dead bat," he says.

Judy is amazed.

Mort himself is at the register, a fat bald man who knows Judy. She tells him she will be going away, he acts as if he will miss her, she acts as if she will miss him, the sorts of things you say.

"Better load your car before this storm hits," he says.

"Oh, I don't have much," says Judy.

The door flips open on its own. They go out past the pile of free TV programs.

"I'm going to Pete's," Judy says at the curb. "If you ever drive down to the beach, look me up." She tells him her address quickly and heads into traffic.

Lou looks at a newspaper in a vending box, a headline about Nicara—— All he can see. He puts two dimes in, opens the box, takes his paper. There is a revolution— He will have to read it. Another headline about tenants' unions. It does not matter, his name is not Tennant. He sees a smaller headline: WOMAN BLEEDS TO DEATH ON SIDEWALK. An old drunk no one helped out— He can use that one to label his doorbell. He will tear off the -DS and have his own real name Blee printed on paper. No one knows that name of his.

Hanno and Niko are on the stoop playing with cards before the storm. Niko has a hat on that says JUNK FOOD. "See my new hat. I have birthday party at last day of school with balloons. Miss Forp give it me well I mean Miss Ththorp."

"Oh God not again," says Hanno, "always pwesents pwesents pwesents."

The cards are laid out in the pattern of the ten.

"I show Hanno the trick. We play on Mama," Niko says. "Very tricky tricky wif with the ten. I figure it out de systame." He looks at the cards, chewing his fingernails. "Mama be so mad she can it not figure."

Tap tap tip tap tip tip tap tap tap tap—

"Dis twick only faw people what is smawt get de point," says Hanno. He is not wearing his gloves. His hands look splotchy but all right.

"See you," Lou says. The door slams behind him. The long creaky stairs up to his place—

28

Lou Blee puts his last name beside the button with a bit of tape he peels off one corner of the scribbled name Alphonse. That time Lew buzzed he must have guessed it was the top button.

The boys are not on the stoop when Lou puts up his name. There is no sound from their door, no sound from the man in back. The wind is blowing in Lou's room. Almost in darkness the morning glory leaves blow wildly across the alley. In there they are watching TV, having their dinners. Good-bye, thinks Lou. He begins to forget them.

He looks at his newspaper with the tiny rectangle torn from the front page. In the upper right the weather says: HIGH WINDS—SUMMER STORM. He puts the paper down messily, the old drunk, the tenants, the revolution. He is tired. It is almost too cold to take off his clothes, but he does. He wants to feel cold.

He looks at his room, empty shelves with the printout flopping over one shelf, newspaper on the floor, clothes thrown about, empty bottles, guitar with a broken string lying on its back in a corner, box of crackers with some eaten, wrapper of the chocolate bar crinkled up. He will not hook up his unhooked curtain tonight. He stands naked in front of the window, but Lew cannot see through the morning glory leaves. Then he flips off the light.

Two rectangles: his window with light from streetlamps, his rug he feels with his toes in the dark— He sits on it, prickly on his bottom, on the bottoms of his thighs. He called it Oblivia. He forgets that it is to remind him of where he was. It is the island he sleeps on now, deep in its green, trees twining into trees, trees behind these trees in a deep forest, black water of the floorboards around it in the dark. He floats there.

If the motorcycles rev up, if cars and trucks pass, if that door flaps, if the man downstairs— The wind is too loud for all that noise or to carry the song from a radio to Lou's ears. The telephone wires snap against the sky. Lou leans forward to the window, kneels at it, chin on the sill. Wind swirls down among the branches of the ailanthus tree. A trash can rolls about in the alley. It is not a cat that has got into it. Cold edges up his arms to his shoulders. His armpits are cold. He crosses his arms in the cold over his chest.

He remembers Kikatu pacing on his branch. The wind blew him off it, or he slipped tangled in his rope. Lou thinks of that place where he was, a forest, a lagoon, piles of shit, why is he forgetting it, and pelicans? Diving?

The edges of the newspaper flip in the wind. The printout blows off the shelf to the floor. Lou gets up to close the window with a slam. The pane keeps rattling, the wind would break it, blow him out.

Sit on the rug— Through the wind it is dark at Lew's. Who was that Lew? When they would talk they were both Lou to anyone listening, or both Lew. Are you cold, Lou? No, Lew, are you? A little cold, not too. It's quiet up here, Lew, not much of a view. Who needs a view, Lou?

Lou makes conversations in his head. He forgets if he is Lou or Lew. He does not see it in his head but hears the sound. We can go for a beer, Loo. I've got a six-pack, Loo, in the cooler. Sounds good, Loo. Is this the life? See you, Loo. Good-bye, Loo. The sound of wind—

Lou does not remember the difference between him and Lew. If he is Lew too— There is no Lew, disappeared into the blue. Lou is Lew. He has forgotten himself too many times. He cannot remember himself again. Lou is to be forgotten. Who knew him? Who was that Lou?

He has drunk a bottle and now another bottle. He does not know who he is. He would fly in the night and howl while the wind is howling. He would bust through the windowpane, walk straight out on the air. The pane rattles.

He stands up, steps to the rug's edge. Hang out there by his fingers, his armpit hair flipping— Who would see him? He leaps at the window busting through it reaching for the wires. But he is hanging off the swirling ailanthus tree with his arms over the branches. It was not that much of a fall.

29

The sun approaches across the creatures in the trees. Yellow pelican bills, brown-skinned little boys laughing, the eyes of coatimundis, their red snarls—

He sees the pattern, all the bills, the eyes, the brown bodies, but only a surface. They climb, perch in the still trees, in trees behind these. The sun makes him see almost into a forest. He has no idea what it is filled with.

He will take his inflatable olive green raft, float between the trees, hear songs from the high branches. The sun shines through the leaves against his eyelids, his Adam's apple, each nipple, warming his paler parts, strongest around his belly button. He squashes mosquitoes on his reddish skin. No thoughts in his head—

He floats through these trees on the summer flood. If he hits a bank he pushes off with a bare foot. He lies on his back with his knees up, neck against the prow, his yellow hair hanging over catching the sun. The water pulls him through the trees, the trees behind the trees, around and back and forth. No one knows him or where he is.